Cara Lockwood is the *USA TODAY* bestselling author of more than seventeen books, including *I Do (But I Don't)*, which was made into a Lifetime Original movie. She's written the Bard Academy series for young adults, and has had her work translated into several languages around the world. Born and raised in Dallas, Cara now lives near Chicago with her two wonderful daughters. Find out more about her at caralockwood.com, 'friend' her on Facebook, facebook.com/authorcaralockwood, or follow her on Twitter, @caralockwood.

If you liked *No Strings*, why not try

One Night Only by JC Harroway
My Royal Sin by Riley Pine
Playing Dirty by Lauren Hawkeye

NO STRINGS

CARA LOCKWOOD

MILLS & BOON

First Published in Great Britain 2018
by Mills & Boon, an imprint of HarperCollins*Publishers*
1 London Bridge Street, London, SE1 9GF

ISBN: 978-0-263-93222-5

MIX
Paper from
responsible sources
FSC C007454

This book is produced from independently certified FSC™ paper
to ensure responsible forest management.
For more information visit www.harpercollins.co.uk/green.

Printed and bound in Spain
by CPI, Barcelona

For PJ, my love and inspiration.

PROLOGUE

Saturday

HE STOOD BEFORE HER, the curve of his bare chest an invitation as he stood in the moonlit hotel suite overlooking the glass high-rises of downtown Chicago. She ran her finger down the firm slope of his well-defined muscles, amazed at their taut perfection. He gently slid the bra strap down off her shoulder, the wisp of his touch setting her skin on fire, and all she could think was: *I don't even know his name. I'm going to let this man do whatever he wants to me, and I have no idea what to even call him.*

She opened her mouth to ask, once more, but he covered her lips with his, and the question of the night evaporated in the heat of animal want. A moan escaped her, as he deftly undid the front clasp, setting her heavy breasts free. He dipped down, expertly flicking a tongue across one nipple, bringing it to attention. He then cupped the other in his strong hand, kneading it with intent.

His mouth is on me and I don't know what he does for a living. I don't even know if he has a dog. Or hell, a wife. I met this man one hour ago. A simple text exchange from an app on my phone. And now I'm here, half naked...

"I—I've never done this before…a stranger, I mean," she murmured. He nibbled her nipple, the flick of teeth on the soft skin making her shiver. "This is… I mean, this is crazy. I don't usually do this."

He straightened, meeting her gaze with his unnervingly perfect hazel eyes. A lazy grin spread across his handsome face, warming up his squared-off jaw. "Even good girls should be bad, once in a while."

She was a good girl. She never did this kind of thing. She'd only ever had sex with two other men her whole life, and both of them after a minimum of three months of dating first, but something about him made her feel reckless. Wild.

"I just can't believe…" She wasn't even sure how she'd gotten here this fast, how she'd met a man and within an hour, was letting him see her everything. To put his hands and his mouth on her body. "I just… I don't know anything about you."

"You having second thoughts?" He paused, hazel eyes fixing her in a locked stare.

"No," she said. No, she wanted him. She did.

He pressed his hard, muscled chest against hers, dipping his face so close their noses nearly touched. "And all you need to know about me is this," he promised. She felt heat rise in her very core. He wanted her as much as she wanted him. And, God, did she want him. She'd wanted this the moment they'd met in the hotel bar an hour ago. She'd decided then in that split second to let him do what he wanted. She was willing.

"You can tell me whatever you want me to do to you. I want you to tell me." She sucked in a breath and her knees trembled slightly. She didn't have to be a good girl. Not with him. She could be bad. Very, very bad. She could do whatever she wanted. She could let him do…whatever he wanted.

She could feel her want, soaking the thin fabric of the lace, the last thin barrier between her and this rash act she was about to commit, this terrible, inconceivably bad thing. Part of her wanted to say no, but her body was in control now. Her body wanted this, wanted it badly, and she became simply an animal in heat, overcome by desire and thousands of years of instinct. For this night, she would give in to her basest desires. There was no turning back now. She was going to give her everything to a man she didn't know, to a perfect stranger. She was going to let him do things to her no man had before.

And she was going to like it.

CHAPTER ONE

The day before

EMMA ALLAIRE STARED at the newly downloaded *Nost* app on her phone and sighed. "You're sure I need to do this?" she asked her best friend, Sarah, once more as they sat together at their favorite brunch place in Lincoln Square, the mild, not quite fall air of mid-September gliding across the open patio as people meandered past them on the busy city sidewalk. *Nost,* short for No Strings, was the latest hookup app that all of her friends were talking about, a place to meet men for casual sex. The app's ominous black logo appeared on her phone and she double-tapped it.

"Em, just give it a shot, okay?" said her gorgeous redheaded friend with the perfect alabaster skin, the curves that didn't quit and the string of musician boyfriends who paraded in and out of her life. "You never know until you try."

"But *this* is what's wrong with us," Emma cried, holding up her phone, to show *Nost*'s loading page. It read, "No names. No strings. 100% fun." She pushed up her black-framed, librarian glasses and scowled at her phone. "How is *anyone* going to find true love *like this*?" She showed Sarah a picture of a shirtless man making a kissing face at a mirror. The app implored her to "swipe right for a good time" or "nope, swipe left."

"Honey, you know this isn't about true love. It's about getting off." Sarah's eyes gleamed.

Emma shrieked a laugh. "What are you *even talking* about?"

Sarah waved her fork in the air. "Wait, you do get off, don't you?"

Emma felt her face flush red. "Um... Yes. I do."

Just, you know, with only two guys. Ever. In her whole dating history, but Sarah didn't need to know that right now.

Sarah pushed up her sunglasses on her nose and leaned back, lifting her face to the fall sunshine coating the small patio of the restaurant. "Good. I thought for a second you were one of those poor souls who'd never had an orgasm."

Emma glanced around the restaurant, suddenly worried someone might overhear. Sarah just shook her head at her friend. "Orgasm!" she cried, louder, and a father of two glanced over at their table and frowned.

"Hush!" Emma commanded. Not that it would do any good. Sarah spoke her mind. Their server appeared then, placing delicious-looking plates of food in front of them. Sarah dug in, while Emma focused on the app.

"*This* is what is wrong with us. Anonymous one-nighters? I mean, you are seriously going to have sex with a man and all you know is his handle is..." Emma peered at her screen. "Hot4U?"

Sarah laughed a little. "Who cares about love when he's got abs like that?" she said, pointing to the man's six-pack.

"And enough tattoo ink on him to write *War and Peace*," Emma pointed out. "He's got *two* arm sleeve tattoos."

"You just have to fuck him, not marry him," Sarah said, rolling her eyes, as she forked a mouthful of spinach quiche into her mouth. "And bad boys are *very* good in bed. Live a little, Em. *Seriously.* You know you settle *too* fast for just about any guy who buys you a drink. Then you end up in a two-year relationship with them while they bore your friends to death."

Emma knew she was talking about Devin, her last boyfriend with the less-than-sparkling personality. He'd been the only other guy she'd seriously dated other than her high school boyfriend.

"Not *all* of my exes are that way."

"You need to *date around.* Hell, *sleep around.* Not just commit to the very first guy who shows up. You know I'm right." Sarah studied her friend.

Emma twirled a loose tendril of hair around her finger and sighed. She glanced down at her flowy, flowered peasant top and her modest jeans and tried to imagine herself meeting up with Mr. Tattoo and taking all her clothes off. She simply couldn't.

"I need romance," Emma declared. "There's no romance in this. This is what *men* want. It's not what women want."

Sarah snorted. "How do you know if you've never tried it?"

"I know that this is just one more way men are manipulating us into thinking that what *they* want is somehow *us* being liberated," said Emma, her women's studies major coming out in blazing good form. "This is just *Girls Gone Wild* in sex app form."

"Em, can you spare me the feminist rant until *after* I've finished my mimosa?" Sarah held up her champagne glass.

"No...this is what I *do* for a living." She wrote freelance stories about women's issues for a women's online magazine, and she had a small but loyal following. "And because clearly you're being manipulated by the patriarchy," Emma declared and grinned. She knew what she sounded like: a militant femi-Nazi. But honestly, she felt like she was the only one who could see it—the fact that the wage gap was still a thing. And that the US was the only industrialized nation not to offer paid maternity leave, and...now there was *Nost.* Like Tinder, but in its most extreme form. The app men didn't have to even *try* to get laid. She was all for the sexual revolution, but not when it meant that the advantage went entirely to men.

"This is just...this is just one more way men have tricked us into getting what *they* want. Sex and no commitment."

"Fine, so delete it," Sarah said, sighing, showing her exasperation, as she finished off the last of her meal. Emma, who had already devoured her blueberry waffle, wondered, not for the first time, how she and Sarah, so total opposites, ever got along. Their random pairing as college roommates had set off an unlikely friendship: Sarah, the impulsive redhead, who never flinched at a dare, and Emma, the bookworm, who one day hoped to run for elected office. If she were honest with herself, finding Mr. Right ranked somewhere between growing her blog readership base and putting money in her IRA. Dating just didn't seem important at the moment—she was just twenty-eight. She had plenty of time. At least, that's what she told herself. After her last disastrous relationship, where her boyfriend, Devin, chose a new job in Seattle over her, she just wasn't too into the idea of putting herself out there again.

"Actually," Sarah said, sipping her mimosa. "You don't even *need* to delete it. Your profile will become invisible to the guys on your screen in forty-eight hours."

"What? Why?"

Sarah put down her fork, and looked exasperated. She flipped her dark red hair off one shoulder.

"Because the whole point of it is *not* to have a relationship longer than that. Every two days, you get a whole new slew of potential guys and the old ones can't find you. Every time, it's new, and the best part is, there's no awkward follow-up. You have sex and then—whoosh!—you disappear. It's ghosting, but the app does it for you. Everybody knows the score. Nobody gets hurt."

Emma put her head in her hands and groaned. "Are you kidding me?" She peeked at Sarah from her fingers. "The profiles become invisible?"

"That's the point," Sarah said. "Wham, bam, thank you, ma'am. Emphasis on the bamming part."

"Sarah! What about rapists? Serial killers?" Emma couldn't believe her friend was even seriously suggesting anonymous sex. Wasn't that beyond sketchy?

"The good ones already have a background check. See that little *v* next to 'Hot4U'? He uploaded a background check. No felonies. *Nost* verified him. So, you don't have to."

Emma blew bangs out of her eyes. "What about… STDs?"

"See that little *c* next to him?"

Emma nodded.

"That means he's been tested in the last month. He's clear."

"I guess they've thought of everything. You know, except real human intimacy."

"Ha. Ha. Very funny. Don't knock it till you try it." Sarah pointed at Emma with her fork.

"Seriously, though, how can you do…this?"

"I'm busy. I work sixty hours a week because those commercial buildings aren't going to sell themselves.

And, yeah, it's kind of hot." She took a swig of her mimosa, finishing it, and glanced back at Emma. "And, a one-night stand? I mean, who hasn't had one of those?"

Emma froze. *She* hadn't, actually. She could never imagine herself getting naked in front of a stranger. She'd only ever had sex with her high school boyfriend, whom she'd dated three years before they'd even had sex, and then her post-college boyfriend, Devin, whom she dated three months before they'd done the deed. How could someone just… jump into bed with a man they'd only just met? By the time she'd had sex with someone she was already emotionally invested, even in love. She couldn't imagine it any other way.

Sarah paused, glancing at her friend and read her expression. "Wait. You've…never?"

Emma felt on the spot, suddenly. Did that make her a prude? From the expression on Sarah's face, the answer was yes. "No. Never."

"Not even…college? I mean, everyone has one then." Sarah leaned forward, her shock evident.

"Not me." Emma took another sip of her mimosa.

"Well, then. You *have* to do this. You can't turn thirty without having *done this.*" Sarah leaned forward. "Look, why don't we make a deal? You try it for forty-eight hours. Go on *one* drink date at least. You don't have to sleep with anybody. But can't you write about it? If it turns out to be so bad, rant about it online for your magazine."

"I don't *rant,*" Emma corrected. "I discuss issues."

"Honey, you *rant*, but that's okay. It's one reason why I love you. You've got opinions and you're not afraid to share them." Sarah leaned forward and patted Emma's hand. "What have you got to lose? You either get laid *or* you get the subject of your next article. Win-win."

Sarah had a point there. And it had been a long time since Devin moved to Seattle.

"So what do I do?" Emma asked, holding up her phone.

"First, you get a better picture than that," Sarah declared, looking at Emma's profile and wrinkling her nose in disapproval. She swiped Emma's phone out of her hand and took her Elvis Costello glasses off in one quick swipe.

"I need those to see!"

"Not now you don't." Sarah clicked a few impromptu shots of Emma at the table.

"No! Don't… I…" Emma laughed a little, as Sarah clicked a few more before stopping.

Sarah swiped through them. "Yes, *that* one." She showed her friend the shot: Emma looking away, mid-laugh, blonde hair loose and cascading down one bare shoulder, her peasant top slipping ever so slightly downward revealing the curve of cleavage. "My shirt is practically falling off!" Emma protested.

"That's the point. News flash: Guys like boobs." Sarah rolled her eyes as she tapped on Emma's phone.

Emma sighed. "Sarah…this is just playing into all the stereotypes…"

"Don't go lecturing me on how you hate being a sex object. *This* is the picture you use. You look like you're fun...and you don't have a stick up your butt."

"I don't!" Emma cried, reaching for the phone. Sarah batted her hand away, typing up her profile. "And what are you doing?"

"Making sure you go through with this." Sarah tapped her screen a few more times, concentrating hard.

"You think all problems can be solved by getting laid."

"Can't they, though?" Sarah grinned, her green eyes sparkling with mischief.

Emma giggled and tried to take back her phone. Sarah ducked deftly. Emma gave up and reached for her coffee mug. "Sarah, come on."

"Fine." Sarah glanced at her friend, the dare unmistakable in her gaze. "It's not live until you hit that button."

Emma glanced at the screen and nearly choked, almost sloshing her coffee. "You called me 'Kitten'?" Inwardly, Emma groaned.

"The sex part is implied," Sarah said, signaling the waiter to refill her mimosa. Emma had a feeling she'd need another one, too. "Just hit the 'get laid' button, and you're good to go." Sarah grinned.

"A 'get laid' button? Seriously?" Emma hesitated. Was she really going to do it? This was so unlike her and yet... *It's just research. How bad could it be?*

"You don't like it, you can delete the app whenever

you want," Sarah said. She studied her friend. "You're not scared are you?"

"Are you seriously peer pressuring me into this?"

"Whatever works." Sarah shrugged.

"Fine." Emma tapped the button, sending her profile live out into the universe, telling random strangers in the Chicagoland area she was willing and available. She wasn't sure quite how she felt about that.

"That's my girl," Sarah said, patting her hand. "See? That wasn't so bad."

"Now what?" Emma glanced at her phone, as if it would suddenly hold all the answers.

"Now you wait." Sarah took a big swig of her mimosa. "Don't worry. You probably won't even hear from anybody for hours—until tonight."

Emma glanced at her empty plate when her phone dinged. The *Nost* app lit up her screen with an incoming message.

"Did I say hours?" Sarah put down her champagne glass. "With your hot self, looks like *you* just had to wait a minute."

Emma's phone dinged once more. And then, a third time.

What have I gotten myself into?

Sarah grabbed her phone. She began scrolling through options. "Nope. No. *Oh, God...no.*" Sarah held up the phone and showed Emma a picture of a man trying to shove a foot-long hot dog in his mouth in one go.

Emma wrinkled her nose. Who would want to have sex with…that?

"I feel like I've just wandered into an ugly bar, and I'm going to spend the next twenty-four hours being harassed."

"Maybe." Sarah flicked through a few more pictures. "Oh my. Here's the man for you." She showed Emma another one, this one of a man in a full Spider-Man suit, his face covered.

Emma barked a laugh. "No, it's not. Look at his… You know." She pointed to the picture's groin where his very little bit was fully outlined for nearly all to see.

"Ew!" Sarah cried and dissolved into giggles. "No baby carrots for you!"

Sarah flicked through a few more. "Oh, this guy is nice. Mr. X? Sounds…intriguing."

"Mr. X? Uh, no." Emma shook her head.

Sarah kept flipping. Then, she stopped on one. "Ooh…he's cute." Sarah showed the screen to Emma and showed a blond, blue-eyed thirty-something in a suit.

"I guess so." Emma shrugged.

"Guess so? He's one hundred percent Christian Grey. And even his name is cute… Happy Fun Time! I am setting this up."

"Sarah!" Emma tried to grab her phone. "Don't!"

"You're on for tomorrow night, at the bar in the Ritz-Carlton downtown."

Emma blew a strand of hair out of her face. “Why did you do that?”

“Because I knew you wouldn’t.”

CHAPTER TWO

EMMA HAD SPENT twenty-four hours trying to figure out a way to cancel this date. But as Sarah had pointed out countless times, it was only a drink. If she didn't like Mr. Happy Fun Time, she could simply walk out of the bar and never talk to him again. Yet, the idea of meeting a man *just for sex*, well, she just didn't know if she'd be able to go through with it, even if she wanted to.

I'm just going to meet him. Have a drink. Then, tell him politely that maybe we could have more dates before we...uh...do it... IF we ever do it and that's a big if.

Emma would need about six dates before she'd even consider taking her clothes off. Maybe twelve. Emma realized with a start that she'd never even had sex with a man she wasn't almost or totally in love with already. When her friends were hooking up in college, she was tied to her high school boyfriend long-distance. Then after college, she began her relationship with Devin. That was before he took a job in Seattle and told her they ought to see other people six months ago.

Emma had thought they'd been headed for marriage, but turns out, she was just headed for...dating apps.

She stood before her closet studying the contents and wondering what on earth she was supposed to wear on this date that was almost, surely going nowhere.

"Hmmm," she muttered, as she pulled out a flowered sundress which screamed summer and wouldn't work for the cool September night she was expecting. Besides, it showed too much leg. *Don't want to give the wrong impression,* she thought. *Oh, wait, I already have, because this is NOST.*

No strings.

She sighed and pulled out a black turtleneck sweater. Maybe she ought to show up wearing this and baggy sweatpants and see whether or not she'd send the shallow Mr. Happy Fun Time running. She grinned to herself, but then decided against it. She put the sweater back in her closet and tried to dig around for something middle of the road. Emma lamented the fact that she was wasting so much mental energy on what she was going to wear on a date that she didn't even want to have in the first place. She ought to be outlining more chapters in that book she planned to write.

She glared at the closet, wishing it was her computer screen.

"I should cancel this date," she told her closet. "I should text him and cancel."

She whipped out her phone and pulled up the *Nost* app. Then Mr. Happy Fun Time's picture came up:

blond, sophisticated suit, like a successful and rich businessman. Well, what could it hurt? Just because his picture looked like something she'd find on a corporate About Us page didn't mean that he was all that stuffy. Maybe he had a sense of humor. Maybe he'd be quick-witted. Maybe he'd just buy me drinks, she thought, as she remembered her less than stellar bank account balance that month. The freelance gigs had been a little less than hot and heavy these last few weeks, and she'd had to lean on credit cards more than she'd like.

I don't need men to buy me anything, she reminded herself. Just because her budget was tight didn't mean that she wasn't a fully functional independent woman. One more reason to cancel. She was already buying into the patriarchy—the idea that this guy in the suit should *buy her a drink.*

Of course, Sarah would say that casual sex proved her independence from men. Emma shook her head. Feminism was complicated. She glanced once more at her closet, grabbed a pair of jeans and one of her favorite off-the-shoulder sweaters and paired it with a pair of ankle boots, no heel. Emma stood five-seven, so she already knew she was better off assuming Mr. Happy Fun Time was shorter than her. Emma didn't care, but she knew men did. It had been her experience that men lied about their height. He said he was five-eleven, but that could mean anything.

She pulled on her outfit, dusted on some light makeup and then checked out her reflection in the mirror. Even she could tell she looked tense, even when she plastered on a fake smile and tossed her blond hair over one shoulder.

This is just research, she told herself. She'd take mental notes and then have a hell of a story to pitch to her editor tomorrow.

She nodded at herself in the mirror, meeting her clear blue-eyed gaze. "One drink," she told herself. "An hour tops."

Emma sat at the upscale bar in the Ritz-Carlton bathed in the fading sunlight of early evening beaming down through the canopy of windows encasing the tastefully decorated lounge. She felt self-conscious as she nursed the Hendrick's and tonic she'd ordered from the bartender and kept checking her phone. Where *was* Mr. Happy Fun Time? He was seven minutes late was what he was. Emma glanced once more around the bar and saw three women chatting happily around a coffee table in the lounge, two men in business suits that were about ten years too old to be Mr. Happy Fun Time *and* both brunettes, and a tourist sitting in the corner in a leather armchair, wearing a St. Louis Cardinals jersey and looking more than a tad underdressed in the swanky bar with the white leather couches and the enclosed-window view of the impressive buildings in Chicago's Loop. She gazed out the window, across the way at the copper-colored windows of the Time Life office building across the street, and wondered how long she ought to stay before abandoning this futile exercise altogether.

Until I finish this drink, she promised herself, as she rattled the ice cubes around the cocktail glass and took another deep sip of the clear liquid. *No date and no story.* She couldn't help but feel a pang of disappointment. Not because she wanted casual sex, but because she had started to like the idea of writing a story about her first *Nost* date. Skewering it relentlessly. She'd already thought of about 500 words she'd like to cram in it about women's self-esteem and respecting yourself and a whole lecture she planned to give about the dangers of embracing casual sex. Feeling someone watching her, she glanced up and saw Cardinals Jersey staring. He had a matching baseball hat, too. Bold move wearing rival team paraphernalia in Chicago. She glanced away and focused on her phone. No messages, no *Sorry, I'm running late*, or anything. Figures. Not like one-night stand seekers cared about manners. Emma studied her drink. Three more sips, probably, and she'd leave.

A new man came to sit in the lounge and she glanced up, hopeful it was Mr. Happy Fun Time, but realized instantly he wasn't. He was much, *much* taller than five-eleven, probably at least six-two, and looked like a former wide receiver with broad shoulders, big hands and thick, muscled arms. He seemed to almost change the atmosphere of the lounge somehow, as everyone took notice of the dark-haired stranger who strode confidently to the bar. He slid into an empty stool at the end of her row and signaled the bartender. That was a man, she thought, his muscles evident even through the thick fabric of his shirt. He was a smidgen older than her. Early thirties, maybe? He had a smooth olive complexion but piercing, hazel eyes, not quite green, almost golden.

Wow, but the man had a body. Trim waist, thick legs. He had to be a professional athlete, she thought. Did she know him? Blackhawks? Cubs? Something. Had to be. A body like that was made to be put to work. That was a body that could make a million-dollar contract, no doubt. Model? Maybe he was a model. Or an action star. Someone from the cast of *Chicago Fire*? Seemed like he had to be famous.

He glanced up for a second, and sent her the smallest quirk of a smile, and that was when she realized she was staring at him like an idiot. She grabbed her phone and glanced down, wondering if he realized she'd been mentally undressing him. Emma felt a blush creep up the back of her neck. *I must have sex on the brain,* she thought. *Look! Nost is already working.*

He was handsome, she admitted to herself as she tried not to openly stare. He had jet-black hair and wore a button-down shirt tucked into dark washed jeans. His arms looked muscled even through the fabric of his shirt, and his stomach was flat and hard, not a hint of unfit abs anywhere. He wore a watch on his wrist that even from a distance looked expensive, but no wedding ring, Emma noticed. The bartender served him a top-shelf rye on the rocks. The man took a sip as he pulled out his phone.

This is why we have to use apps all the time, Emma lamented. *We don't see who's right in front of us.*

It reminded Emma of the time her mother asked her why she didn't just go out with her friends to meet someone. *This was why,* she inwardly groaned. All the best prospects kept their noses in their phones. Her own phone dinged with an incoming alert, and she grabbed it from the bar. Maybe it was Mr. Happy Fun Time.

She glanced at her phone and saw a message from *Nost* all right, but it hadn't come from Happy Fun Time. It had come from "Mr. X," the same profile that had popped up earlier yesterday. Emma saw a timer already going on the profile signaling how much time she had to reply. Emma also noticed he had both a *v* and *c* next to his name: verified and clear, she remembered. Good. That was good.

Just wanted to say hi, since you're in my neighborhood.

Neighborhood? Huh?

How did you know that? She typed quickly, glancing around, almost as if she'd find someone staring at her.

The maps feature? He offered.

Emma literally smacked her own forehead. Of course. The "who's closest to me on *Nost* right now" map. Or, as she liked to think about it, the *I have to get laid right now and anybody will do, ANYBODY in a one square mile area* feature. She glanced at the map and saw the markers and realized about a dozen *Nost* users were in the vicinity, hell, the very building she was in. *But I'm in a hotel, so duh.* She tried to figure out where Mr. X might be, but couldn't quite make it out. There were so many little triangles, they all overlapped in one big blob.

What does Mr. X stand for? she asked.

X factor. Of course. Besides—Tall Dark and Handsome was already taken.

She had to grin. Confidence was sexy. She took a look at his picture. Wow. Mr. X only just scratched the surface. Jet-black hair…amazing hazel eyes…smooth complexion with just the hint of stubble on his strong chin. He looked vaguely familiar. Why did he look so familiar?

A new message popped up from Mr. X.

Want to grab a drink? You're right here. As in…literally… right here.

She felt the heavy weight of a stranger's gaze on her. She glanced up and saw Mr. Must Be Famous raising his glass in her direction. Mr. X…was *him.* A shock of surprise and delight ran through her. The gorgeous man next to her was on…*Nost.* Well, maybe Sarah had been right. Maybe this wasn't such a crazy idea after all.

He was even better looking than his profile picture, and his profile picture was darn near perfect. Mr. X flashed a bright white smile and Emma felt her stomach tighten. Would she join him for a drink? She was sorely tempted. Maybe she should. What did she have to lose?

Emma grabbed her drink and caught movement from the corner of her eye. She hoped it was Mr. X, but instead, she turned to see the tourist in the Cardinals getup standing right in front of her, blocking her path. He sent her a goofy, bent-toothed smile and she grabbed her phone.

"Hey." The tourist plopped down on the stool next to hers. He had some nerve, especially since he was decked out head to toe in her least favorite team of all time. Her family had been die-hard Cubs fans for as long as she could remember. She was sure if she lived in St. Louis, she'd have a closet full of Cardinals jerseys, but even she wouldn't be rude enough to wear one deep in enemy territory. Plus, he had to be…fiftyish? Her dad's age? Older? He certainly carried a lot of extra weight, too. And were those white sneakers he was wearing? And white socks. She felt a creep of revulsion down the small of her back. Ugh. Just…ugh.

"Uh…oh. Hi." Emma glanced up briefly and then tried to look for Mr. X, over his shoulder. Mr. X frowned, clearly annoyed by the interruption, but he calmly took a sip of his drink. Mentally, Emma sent him a *what's up with this dude?* vibe.

Emma didn't want to be rude, but…she really didn't want to talk to the tourist. She knew that probably made her one of the snobby city folk her relatives were always complaining about, but sheesh. He was wearing a Cardinals baseball hat deep in Cubs territory. Plus, who wore a baseball cap to the Ritz-Carlton?

"Are you…Kitten?"

Emma froze. Her *Nost* name. "How did you…" She glanced once more at the man, who had a day's worth of stubble on his double chin. He looked like no picture she'd seen on the app. And she'd flipped through plenty.

"I'm Happy Fun Time."

Emma could feel all the blood drain out of her face. *This* guy, this older…much heavier-set guy, with the white tube socks, looked literally nothing like his picture because she realized he'd used a photo of someone else.

He grinned, showing crooked, yellowed teeth. And, she got the whiff of stale cigarette smoke. Ugh. If the Cardinals jersey wasn't enough of a deal breaker, this would be. For sure.

"You look *just* like your picture," he said, beaming, looking pleased.

That's because I'm actually in my picture, she wanted to say but didn't.

"So, I got us a nice hotel room…"

Emma's jaw dropped. "Here?" she squeaked, glancing at his worn sneakers. How could he afford a room at the Ritz-Carlton?

"Oh, God, no," he said, shaking his head. "Can't afford here. There's a Motel 6, just off the expressway a little ways out of town. If we get in my car now…"

Emma suddenly had visions of duct tape and chloroform. She tried to get Mr. X's attention, but now he had his eyes on his phone. Argh. She wondered if he was scouting the room for other *Nost* possibilities.

"Look…you've gotten the wrong idea," she said, trying to be nice but firm. There was no way she was going anywhere with this guy. No way. He needed to leave. She needed to go to Mr. X. *That* was a *Nost* date she wouldn't mind.

But Mr. Happy Fun Time stood, and reached out to grasp her elbow. She tugged her arm away, just out of his reach. No way was he *touching* her.

"What's the problem, baby?" He moved closer to her and the acrid scent of burnt tobacco got stronger.

She actually leaned back away from him, fighting the urge to flat-out flee.

"Look, you seem nice, but I don't think there's a connection. I think…" *You are totally disgusting and you put up a bogus picture and there's no way I'm going to spend five minutes with you, much less an evening.*

Happy Fun Time frowned. "You said you wanted to meet." He acted as if that entitled him to see her naked.

"Yes, but…"

"So, what's your problem? You a tease?" His voice had an edge to it now, and suddenly she realized that he was much bigger and heavier than her. If he wanted, he could sling her over his shoulder and carry her out of here. Emma felt a tingle of dread in the pit of her stomach, that little instinct that told her *Careful. Something's off here.*

Emma glanced at the bartender, but he was at the other end getting drinks. The other patrons were busy with their own conversations. All except Mr. X, who studied her. Thank God. He was tuned into the situation once more. Would he do something? She met his gaze. He quirked an eyebrow, and she only thought one word: *help.*

At least someone might notice if this guy dragged her out by her hair.

Emma tried to flash Happy Fun Time a conciliatory smile. "I'm sorry," she said, though she wasn't the least bit sorry. "But, I just don't think there's a spark between us. It's just…uh, not going to work."

His frown deepened, and he stood there, seething, looming over her.

"Bitch." The word came out hard and cold and so low she almost wasn't sure if she heard it.

"I'm sorry?" Emma blinked fast. She wasn't used to open hostility.

"You heard me." The look in his eyes was flat, cold, devoid of all emotion. Now she knew something was really off. *Danger*, her instincts screamed. This man was dangerous. Still, she wasn't going to back down. And, had he called her a *bitch*? For what, for saying no?

Now anger flared in her chest. She slid off her bar stool and faced him.

"You need to go. Now." She might be half his size,

but she wasn't about to let this guy push her around. No means no, and right now, she was saying *hell, no.*

He blinked at her, rage building in his cold blue eyes. Was he going to do something? Her heart thudded in her chest. What would she do if he did?

The whole bar seemed to go quiet, even though nobody else moved a finger to do anything. Emma felt suddenly that this man intended to hurt her, and he didn't care who was watching.

"I asked you to go," Emma told the man, voice lower this time, but still firm. *Be calm. Be firm. Don't let him know he's scaring the hell out of you.*

That's when the furious man before her grabbed her arm, hard. "I don't think so." He squeezed and she let out an unintended cry. Panic gripped her as she felt the darkness in him; her instincts were right. This man wanted to hurt her. She tried to wiggle out of his grasp.

"Let the lady go." Mr. X stood behind the man, his voice low but clear.

CHAPTER THREE

THE MAN WHIRLED, off guard. Her savior was about five full inches taller and far more in shape. The two men might weigh the same, but Happy Fun Time's weight came in fat, while Mr. X was pure working muscle. He could wipe the floor with him, and both men knew it. The now angry Happy Fun Time frowned, but backed up a step, releasing Emma's arm.

"We were just talking," he said, defensive.

"Didn't look like a very nice talk to me." Mr. X was all business, eyes serious, shoulders tense. Emma wouldn't want to be on the other end of that angry gaze. She glanced from one man to the other, her heart still thudding hard in her chest, her mind going a million miles a minute.

"You're not worth the trouble," her assailant said, and glared at her, eyes full of menace as he turned and walked quickly out of the lounge and past the lobby. Emma watched him go, feeling a sudden whoosh of relief as she exhaled the tension she'd been holding. That was so close.

"Wow…uh, thank you," she managed to say, grateful now for the backup. Her savior studied her with hazel eyes flecked with gold.

"You okay?" He reached out and touched her elbow, ever so softly. Emma rubbed her arms self-consciously. "I'm sorry I didn't come over sooner… I thought…well, I thought maybe you'd planned the date."

She sighed, still feeling her hands tremble with adrenaline and fear. "I had, but that's the last time I *ever* make a date with someone from *Nost.*"

Her rescuer cocked an eyebrow. "He's on *Nost?* What's his name?"

"Happy Fun Time."

Mr. X frowned. "Not so happy or fun."

"Agreed," she said. "Ugh. Why did I even *try* this? I knew it was a mistake." She sank her head in her hands.

"We're not all bad on *Nost*...Miss *Kitten."* Mr. X grinned. "Come on, let me make up for that asshole. At least let me buy you a drink."

Emma felt shaken, and a drink was desperately what she needed. A drink, and a bit of time to stare at those golden eyes a bit longer. "Sure," she said, though her body felt wired—nerves, fear, all the *fight or flight* chemicals buzzing through her veins. Her heart still thumped in her ears and she felt shaky, but she gestured to the empty bar stool. Having his big body next to hers felt good right about now.

He slid onto the bar stool next to hers and she felt his presence, broad, next to her. The two buttons undone at his neck revealed smooth, bare skin. She was so thankful for him at that moment, she wanted to throw her arms around his neck and squeeze.

"What can I get you?" he asked her, and she felt the gravelly baritone in her stomach.

She felt the heat in her face intensify as her thoughts instantly went to naughty places. *What can't he get me?*

"Hendrick's and tonic," she managed to answer, suddenly feeling shy. What was wrong with her? She'd never felt this kind of instant attraction, the strong pull of basic, animal magnetism before. Sure, she'd found guys handsome, but this one…she could feel his strength, his pull. Every slight shift he made with his body she felt in hers, keenly aware of even the tiniest of movements. Mr. X signaled the bartender, his tanned and muscled forearm raised. He had solid hands. Strong hands. Big ones. Emma imagined what they'd feel like on her body and felt a current of electricity run down her spine. The entire effect just made her feel more rattled, more unsettled, yet in the best way possible.

This must be just adrenaline, she told herself. A dangerous experience, coupled with a handsome guy. *That's all.* It was just hormones and chemicals in her blood, making her aware of this man's every move.

The bartender brought the drink but she barely noticed. She was glancing at his flat stomach and the curve of his chest muscles beneath his shirt. What would the weight of him feel like on top of her?

"Are you okay?" he asked once more. He reached out

and grabbed her hands. She glanced up at him, shaken from her thoughts. “You’re trembling,” he said, voice low with concern, his eyes never leaving hers.

He squeezed both hands tightly. “That jerk is gone. He won’t bother you again.” Mr. X made it sound like a promise. “You’re safe now.”

Emma glanced down at his strong hands covering hers. Why did she feel anything but safe at that moment?

“Thank you,” she said, her heart filling with gratitude. He raised his glass.

“To a better evening,” he said and grinned.

“To a better evening,” she echoed, and they clinked glasses.

Xavier Pena sipped at his drink and gazed at the beautiful blonde sitting next to him. Gorgeous, blue eyes, streaks of spun gold in her blond hair, her skin still tanned from the summer sun. From her thin frame and taut muscles, he would guess she worked out. Ran maybe? She had the body of a triathlete, someone who took her fitness seriously. Just like he did. All the men at the bar—single or attached—noticed this woman, tall, lithe, strong. He’d noticed her the second he’d walked into the bar, and when he’d pulled up *Nost,* was gleefully happy she’d had a profile.

Part of him was surprised to find her there at all. A woman as drop-dead gorgeous as this one shouldn’t need an app to find a date. Or anonymous sex. Any man in this bar would be happy to oblige her, and yet…that was the beauty of *Nost.* Xavier remembered the hard grilling the investors had given him over the concept, especially because they thought women wouldn't want to participate.

"But women have the most to gain from this app," he'd told them. "It gives them a background check *and* allows them to shop for the best mate, without having to weed through suitors at a bar. Women are going to find out that this is exactly what they've been looking for."

It turned out, Xavier had been right. While men slightly edged out women on *Nost,* it wasn't by much.

Xavier sipped at his whiskey and watched the beautiful woman next to him. She'd begun to relax a little. He studied the curve of her bare shoulder, revealed by her off-the-shoulder navy blue sweater. He'd been more than glad to scare off Mr. St. Louis, a man who had no business being in the same room with this woman, much less talking to her. He shouldn't be anywhere near *Nost,* either, a fact he filed away for later. He'd created the app as a fun and *safe* place for women. That was why he'd written in all the background checks. Without the safety net, the app would be a playground for predators, which would be unacceptable. He made a mental note to bring up the user at the next board meeting. They might need to tweak some of their safety checks.

Now he focused on the woman before him. She was more than a pretty face. He suspected there was a lot going on behind those intelligent blue eyes.

He wondered if she felt the little current of *whatever this was* floating between them. The strong physical connection. The *I feel like we've met before* feeling. Xavier had only felt this once or twice before, once with his now ex-fiancée, Sasha.

The minute he thought about her he pushed memories of her away. They were too painful. They were the whole reason he and a group of his fraternity brothers had created *Nost* in the first place. The little app had exploded over the last few weeks, taking them from a bunch of largely unknown software engineers to being propositioned by Google and Facebook for potentially millions. Xavier had nearly the whole world at his feet, but all he wanted was a little companionship. *Temporary companionship,* he reminded himself. He thought of Sasha, her dark eyes and cocoa skin, the way she tilted her head back when she laughed, how much she reminded him of his own mother. His mother who died when he was a kid. Sasha used to have him wrapped around her little finger. That was…until he found out she betrayed him.

He didn't need more pain. Not now. Probably not ever.

Concentrate on the now. The future is too painful. That's why you live in the moment, he reminded himself.

"So…was that really your first date from *Nost*?" he asked her, which was his way of prying without prying. He got why anonymous sex wasn't for everybody. Newbies were a wild card. But he wasn't about putting pressure on anyone. You were in or out, as far as he was concerned.

He watched the color bleed into her cheeks. "Yep. Happy Fun Time was it. Just signed up yesterday…and not sure it's for me. My friend Sarah actually insisted I try it. But…I don't know. I'm a little skeptical. What's in it for women?"

"Oh, everything, actually," Xavier said, raising his glass to his lips. "You'd be surprised."

She quirked an eyebrow, clearly intrigued, as she set her own glass back on the bar, and played with the small black straw, pushing the slice of lime around her cup. "Casual sex was invented by men."

"I don't know about that. Women want just as many partners as men do, you know. It's just that society tells them they should be good girls. But that's all just a construct, really, something *men* want."

"You're saying men want women to have fewer partners," she challenged.

"Of course. Men want it both ways: they want to have sex with as many women as possible, but keep most women at home, under wraps. A fully realized sexual woman who isn't afraid to go after what she needs terrifies most men."

A small blush crept up her pale cheek, which Xavier found a little bit adorable.

Definite newbie. Xavier had more than a handful of women who claimed they'd never consider *Nost*, who suddenly wound up in his bed. And it wasn't just his imposing physique. He knew that anonymous sex could be freeing. If you let the concept in.

"I write for *Helena,* the women's online magazine?" He knew it and nodded. "I kind of thought this would all just be fodder for my next article."

"Ah, so you're going to tell your readers how terrible and sexist the whole thing is," he teased.

"N-no," she countered. "I mean, I was going to research it and…"

"But you'd made up your mind before you even tried it," he said, reading her like the open book she was.

"Maybe." She stirred her drink once more, focusing on the ice cubes there. "And Happy Fun Time didn't help."

"Don't let him be the poster child for your experience," Xavier said. "Believe me, he's the exception not the rule."

"So what do you do for a living?" she asked him, blue eyes intent on an answer. She was a seeker, a collector of facts, someone who wouldn't rest until she got all the information.

"Work in tech," he said, and shrugged. He glanced at the melting ice cubes in his glass.

"Where?"

"Here and there." He grinned. It was the truth. He'd worked at other companies before founding *Nost.* He'd had a lot of practice not revealing details about himself. He'd made that mistake in the past, letting on where he'd worked, and a woman found him through a Google search with only his first name and *Nost.* She stalked him, showing up at work, at his apartment, asking for a relationship he wasn't willing to give. He'd been up front with her, but after two nights with him…she'd fallen for him. It had been a whole mess, actually. Now he'd learned to be more careful. He knew exactly what to reveal—and what to keep secret. He had his rules.

"Tell me more about this article," he said, deftly changing the subject as he deflected interest away from him. "Am I changing your mind about *Nost*?"

She glanced up at him. "Not sure yet," she said. "I'm Emma, by the way."

"X," he replied, and she laughed a little. He never gave his name anymore. Not after the other woman found him.

"No, really."

"Seriously—that's what my friends call me." *Because Xavier is too much of a mouthful for most.* "But, also, no names, it just makes it simpler. On *Nost.*"

"So I should just call you Mr. X?" Emma giggled at the idea. "What are you, a comic book villain?"

Xavier leaned in closer and got a whiff of her perfume…white flowers? Something light and floral. "That depends. Do you like bad boys?"

Now Emma just threw her head back and laughed. The sound was all light and air—music to Xavier's ears. The only thing he loved more than making a woman laugh was making her come.

"No. Not usually. I'm the strictly nice guy type."

"How's that working out for you?" Xavier sloshed his whiskey around the ice cubes in his glass, still studying her perfect cheekbones, and the lovely tilt of her chin. He wanted to kiss the tiny dimple that lay there.

She self-consciously played with a strand of her hair, and glanced at him sideways. Her eyes sparkled just a little. She was flirting with him. He was one hundred percent sure.

"Not that great," she admitted. "All the nice guys I've dated ended up being…not so nice." She frowned, her full, pink lips falling into a pout that could drive most men wild. "My last boyfriend decided a promotion was more important than me. He took the job across the country without even talking to me about it first."

"Maybe you should just start with a bad boy and then you know what you're getting." Xavier flashed a grin and Emma laughed.

"Maybe," she conceded. "Why are you on *Nost*?"

Her eyes probed him for an answer. This was the journalist at work, he realized. He liked the fire in her, the curious intelligence in her blue gaze. She wasn't like the other women he'd met recently. This one thrived on information. Keeping it from her would be a challenge, but one he'd happily accept.

"I love women," he said. "Sex for me isn't about me, it's about them. I can't be satisfied…unless they are. There's nothing more beautiful…or more humbling than giving a woman pleasure." To him, this was absolute truth. Nothing satisfied him more than seeing a woman, head back, mouth open, lost in ecstasy. Knowing that he brought her there.

Emma shifted uncomfortably in her seat and rattled her drink. “But don’t you want…more? Don’t you want love and…a real relationship and all of it?”

“I used to want that. I had that,” he said, feeling a wave of sadness that was stronger than he expected. “I was engaged last year. But…” He thought of Sasha, of finding the passionate text messages she’d sent to another man, of the photos she’d sent wearing the lingerie *he’d* bought her. Those images would be seared into his brain forever. “I found out she’d been sleeping with someone else. Actually, a lot of someones.” He took a long sip of his whiskey, the alcohol leaving a distant burning sensation down his throat. “I’d never been so blindsided. So…heartbroken.” He shrugged. “I guess I’m just not ready for any of that, anything more serious. Not right now. Maybe not ever.”

“She did a number on you,” Emma said, her blue eyes sad, empathy radiating from them.

He nodded and shrugged.

“What was her name?”

“Sasha,” he said, almost at the level of a whisper. “I thought she was the one.” He remembered her dark eyes, her throaty, sexy laugh. The fact that she’d been so free in bed, willing to try anything, game for whatever he asked. Turned out, he wasn’t the only one she was free with.

“But she wasn’t.”

"No," he said, biting off the word, eager to stop talking about Sasha. "But what about you? Why *don't* you like the idea of *Nost*?"

Xavier moved closer, and their knees touched. Emma didn't move away. He took that as a good sign.

She swooped her long, shaggy blond bangs from her forehead. "It seems like it's just what men want. Not what women want. Women want commitment, they want relationships..."

"Yes, with the right man, but what about the freedom to indulge in a fantasy, to play with someone who's *not* the right man, but then walk away the next day? There's something *more* liberating in that for women than men." Now Xavier felt like he was right back in front of the venture capitalists, telling them why *Nost* was worth their time, and more importantly, their money. "Look, women choose. They always choose. We men? We're powerless over that. We wait for you to decide. The power's all yours."

Emma rested her chin on her elbow and cocked her head to one side. "You think?" She shifted a little, so that their knees and legs touched. They were side-by-side now, elbows almost touching on the bar.

"Sure. You decide who's fit enough, strong enough, alpha-male enough. Every decision women make about men is based on that immense responsibility—those thousands of years of you being the ones bearing the reproductive cost and the future of the species. That's a lot of responsibility. But how are you supposed to *know* who's right for you, who's the perfect man, if you *don't* play around? What if the man you always thought was perfect for you wasn't, because you'd never allowed yourself to date outside that very confining box?"

She sent him a lopsided smile. "You're saying I need to sleep around with bad boys to find a good one."

He was aware of the feel of her thigh against his, the heat coming from her. "You need to know what it is you want. How are you supposed to know that without experimenting a little?"

"But, it's all so impersonal... How are you supposed to find something real when it's all just fake?"

"Oh, it's far from fake," he said with a strong shake of his head. "People can often have their most authentic connections when they're with strangers. You don't have to worry about what the other person might think, or if you'll hurt their feelings or how you might be judged. You can be your *real* self because you aren't worried about the future. You're just living in the now."

"Is that right?" Emma still seemed a little skeptical.

"Sure," he said, taking another sip of his drink, which was now three-quarters gone. "For instance, you can tell me anything you want. You can be a hundred percent honest. We probably won't see each other again after this night."

"Okay..." Emma hesitated.

"So, in that spirit, say you do sleep with me tonight." Xavier leaned in closer.

Emma barked a laugh and ran a nervous hand through her hair. “Aren’t you a little overconfident?”

“Maybe,” he said, even though at this point, he thought she’d have to feel the pull between them, the magnetism that drew them together. “But, just indulge me in a little theoretical. Say we do fall into bed tonight. Say we go upstairs into this room.” He pulled out a hotel key card and laid it flat on the bar. Emma glanced at it, intrigued. *Tread carefully,* he told himself. “Which, by the way, is completely and totally up to you. But if we did…what’s the first thing you want me to do to you?”

CHAPTER FOUR

THE KEY CARD ON the bar *and* his question sent a thrill through Emma. What did she want him to do to her? Short answer: *Everything.*

She felt her throat go dry. She had a hard time concentrating when Mr. X leaned in so close to her. His strong chin, the unwavering golden-eyed gaze. The thick jet-black hair that she badly wanted to put her hands in. She glanced at the Ritz-Carlton key card on the bar. That was it. The key to a room upstairs where… where…she could indulge in…him. That squared-off, strong chin, the barely-there stubble, those full, sensual lips. All she could think about was how he'd taste if she kissed him, how those lips would feel on hers. The attraction felt palpable, as if it was a physical law of nature that couldn't be denied, like gravity. Emma realized the absurdity of this situation: that just minutes ago she'd dismissed Happy Fun Time in an instant, but X was different. Calm, collected, confident. Emma couldn't remember the last time she'd felt this kind of pull, this kind of attraction. It had been instantaneous the minute he'd walked into the bar. She'd been aware of him every second, every little move he made.

And the more she learned about him, the more intrigued she became. He had loved deeply before. She saw it in the hurt on his face. He was a complicated man, and as much as she hated to admit it, she loved complicated.

He studied her, waiting for her answer, and she felt the weight of his golden gaze. For the first time since signing up for this ridiculous app, she almost felt *tempted.* What would it be like to follow this man up to a room and…?

"If we went upstairs right now…" He leaned closer, so their elbows were now touching on the bar. "What's the first thing you'd want? This would be a night for you. So…?"

She stared at his full lips.

"A k-kiss?" she offered.

He let out a low chuckle, and she felt the reverberations in her toes. She loved how he laughed—almost like a sensual growl. "You're still behaving like you can't be one hundred percent honest with me. You can. You don't have to tell me the answers you think I want to hear." He studied her. "What did you want your last boyfriend to do…that he'd never do?"

Emma thought about her predictable, staid boyfriend, Devin. He'd never been interested in how she felt about sex. It was always quick, the same position, with him coming in about two minutes, just when she was starting to get warmed up. Emma blamed herself: she never complained about it, and they'd just got stuck in this terrible kind of rhythm. But she didn't know how to talk about it without hurting his feelings, so she didn't.

Now Mr. X was waiting for her answer. And why not be honest? After all, he was right: they probably would never meet again. Even if they didn't have sex tonight, what did she have to lose?

"He never let me…come first." As soon as the words were out of her mouth she felt a little bit lighter. Admitting that—the first time she'd admitted it to anyone—felt like a burden had been lifted. Like she'd finally let go of a dirty secret.

Mr. X stared at her. "He always came first?" He looked shocked, even bewildered as his dark eyebrows knitted together in confusion.

She nodded and took another drink of her gin and tonic, the second cocktail heading to her head with rapid speed. She felt pleasantly light-headed, but didn't know if that was the Hendrick's or Mr. X's eyes on her.

Her experience limited, Emma thought maybe that was how it went with most men: they'd do what they wanted first, and then if they had the energy left over, they'd handle the woman's needs.

"That's unacceptable." The finality of his tone sent another little thrill through her. "I'd make sure you came at least three times."

"Three times?" She nearly spit out her drink. "That's a lot."

"Not nearly enough." He grinned, and his bright white smile in his tanned face seemed blinding. "But we'd have *all* night."

"All night?" Devin subscribed to the one and done philosophy. She doubted sex had ever lasted for her longer than about twenty minutes, and that was a marathon.

"And, of course, all positions. We have to find the one that's right for you." A teasing smile tugged at the corner of his full mouth.

Emma felt the blush inch its way up her neck. She wasn't even sure she *knew* all the positions. The thought was a bit naughty...and a bit thrilling. She was beginning to see the allure of anonymous sex. She wouldn't have to worry about what she looked like from certain vantage points, a concern that nearly always plagued her, or whether or not she ought to suck in her stomach. X was a stranger, and would remain a stranger, so why worry about... any of the normal things she worried about?

She ran her finger around the lip of her glass. "I'm beginning to see why women would want to fall into bed with you right when they meet you."

He leaned in, his voice barely a whisper. "Well, I can tell you this. If you do, you won't be disappointed." She felt the warmth of his breath on her ear and the delicious naughtiness of the whole situation delighted her. She liked flirting—scratch that—loved flirting with this man. She even found herself seriously considering his proposition.

"Somehow, I believe you."

"You should." His confident gaze never left her. He slowly reached out and took her hand. He held it palm up, running a strong finger down her life line. "I like to start slowly. Explore you. Like so." His delicate, featherlike touch sent electric sparks darting upward. Goose bumps ran up her arm. "Every woman is different, and I'd spend a lot of time finding out how unique you are."

"Just how *many* women have you…" She figured probably hundreds. With eyes like that and a body that seemed ready for an underwear ad. She thought he probably got laid anytime he wanted it. Women lining up on *Nost* to have a drink date.

He cocked his head to one side, looking coy. "I've had my share."

Now he was so close to her that when she looked up, she almost felt like she could fall into his gaze, a pool of hazel with flecks of gold. So close to him, she inhaled his spicy sweet scent, like cinnamon with a hint of some woodsy aftershave. He looked good. Smelled good. *I wonder if he tastes good, too.*

The thought jolted her.

"I'm not usually so impulsive."

"Why not?" He wasn't being flippant, she could tell. He really wanted to know.

"I don't know. I guess I worry about what people will think." There, she'd said it. It was her dirty little secret: she cared about other people's opinions. She spent a great deal of time writing in her articles about how women need to believe in themselves and be independent, and yet, she feared the weight of judgment herself.

And was she falling into the trap of believing that women who sleep around, who have casual sex, were somehow less than the ones who were more particular? That little feminist thread would have her head spinning for days.

"No one has to know," Mr. X said simply, as if this answered everything.

"But what if I want to write about it?" she asked. And part of her did. This little drink date was bringing up all kinds of feelings in her: Was she wrong to assume casual sex just benefited men? Should she try to find out? Why did her gut tell her to lean forward right now and kiss this man she'd just met?

"Then, do. I promise to give you something worth writing about." He was so confident, so sure. And part of her knew he was telling the truth. She couldn't imagine sex with this man being anything other than amazing. She could almost feel the electricity zapping between them. He was so close now that if she leaned forward, even slightly, their lips would touch. She held eye contact, unable to break it, caught in a kind of trance. He inched forward and she felt in that instant, he was going to kiss her. Suddenly, she got cold feet. Was he going to kiss her right here at the bar? Was she ready for where that kiss might lead?

She pulled away, ever so slightly. He paused, studying her face. Then, he let her hand go and leaned back. He smiled at her, gently.

"I think I want…I don't know…a real connection," she admitted. This was true. She wanted the whole package: amazing sex *and* love, but what she wanted above all else was a true connection. Something that meant something. Could she get that in one night?

He nodded. "You're not ready," he declared as a statement of fact.

"I'm…" Was he right? She felt all sorts of hormones rushing through her body, nerves tingling along her arms and up the back of her legs. She wanted love, but would she take sex right now in this moment?

"It's okay." He squeezed her hand. "*Nost* isn't for everybody."

That almost sounded like a goodbye. Was he abandoning the chase?

"I make it a rule never to pressure women," he said and shrugged, as he finished the last bit of his drink in his glass and signaled the bartender for his tab. "This is something you want or you don't."

But...wait. I haven't decided. Not yet. Maybe I do want this. The inner admission shocked her.

He signed the check and tucked his credit card back into his expensive leather wallet. "Emma, you're an amazing and beautiful woman and it's been my pleasure sharing this time with you." He took her hand and kissed it, lingering a little over it, his lips soft and gentle.

She still felt shock. Was he leaving? Was this it? But she didn't want the night to end. She didn't want him to walk out of her life and never come back. This connection between them, it had to be real, didn't it? He had to feel it, too?

"Can I…call you?"

He slowly shook his head. "I think we want different things."

Did they? All she knew in that moment was that she didn't want him to leave.

He stood, showing again how tall he was as he towered over her, and then he leaned over and gently kissed her cheek. She felt the warmth of his soft lips pressed against her skin and her stomach tightened. *Don't go,* she willed him. *Don't.*

"Goodbye, Emma," he whispered in her hair.

CHAPTER FIVE

EMMA SAT THERE stunned as she watched Mr. X turn away from her. "Wait," she said, and snaked out and grabbed his arm. She felt the strong muscles of his biceps contract. Wow, they were thick. And strong. She wondered what they'd be like wrapped around her. He stopped, and turned.

"Yes?" The single word held a question, an unspoken dare.

"Maybe I am ready." The words came out in a low whisper.

Mr. X leaned closer to her, putting his body between her and his bar stool. "Maybe?" He quirked an eyebrow. "Maybe doesn't sound very definite."

She inhaled his spicy sweet scent, suddenly feeling light-headed. Still seated, she stared directly at his chest, his taut pecs outlined beneath this cotton shirt. She had to crane her neck to meet his gaze.

"I am. I am ready."

"You sure? This has to be your idea, not mine. You have to want this."

"I do. I do want this." She had the strong urge to put her hands on his chest, feel the firm muscles there. His sensual mouth was so close to hers now that she tilted her head up and grabbed the front of his shirt. Before she realized fully what she was doing, she'd reached up and kissed his lips, ever so gently. The soft, gentle touch of her lips on his sent hormones buzzing through her brain. It was just a peck, but a sensual one, carrying the promise of more to come. Instantly, she felt herself grow hot and cold. He stood very still, as she pulled away once more, suddenly feeling like there were no other people at the bar.

Emma surprised even herself. Normally, she was never so forward, never so…aggressive. She'd never been the first to kiss a man at a bar like this. Yet, Mr. X made her want to do things that…she never had before.

Mr. X cocked his head to one side, studying her, the intensity of his gaze almost feeling like a heavy weight. She blinked fast.

"I see. Well, you have to trust me. Do you trust me?" He studied her, his expression serious, as he reached out, under the bar, and gently laid his hand on her hip, resting it there. The touch sent a current through her, a delicious current. Then, he moved his hand back to the waistband of her jeans and tucked a single finger down the small of her back. She gasped a little, as he ran his finger along the top edge of her lacy black thong, the gesture containing a promise for things to come.

She swallowed, hard, and nodded. He tugged hard

at her waistband and she felt the pressure between her legs. She let out a little gasp. "I—I do. I do trust you."

"Good. Let's go." He handed her the key card to the room. Her heart beat wildly. Was she going to do this? Going to go up with this man she *just* met, this gorgeous, handsome man with the golden eyes? She looked at him and saw more than just a handsome man: she felt a connection with him. He'd been brokenhearted, and she could almost feel that pain in him. She wanted to heal him, somehow, because it was as if they'd met before now. The connection, the pull, she felt to him was real. Not just lust. Something more.

"Okay." She slipped her hand in his and followed him as he led her out of the bar. Every fiber of her being stood at attention: she was going to soon be in this man's arms. This stranger's arms. Doing things she usually reserved for the twelfth date. She met the bartender's gaze as they passed. Did he know? Did all the people in the bar know? Emma felt a little thrill then. The thrill of doing something naughty, something risky, something…she never thought she'd do. She watched his broad shoulders moving a little bit ahead of her, as he led her to the elevators and pushed the up button. The elevators dinged, and Emma felt the sound in her belly. Was she doing this? Oh, God. She was going to do this.

The elevators slid open, and a bellhop, pushing a cart of luggage, stepped out.

"Excuse me, miss," he said, and he gave her a half smile. Did he know, too? What she was about to do?

She felt delicious guilt run through her. She almost felt that everyone knew. Mr. X squeezed her hand and she glanced up at him as they moved inside the empty elevator and he pushed the top button.

As soon as the elevator doors slid shut, he'd pulled her into his arms and covered her mouth with his. The pent-up attraction of the last hour exploded then as he devoured her mouth and she responded in kind, her mind overwhelmed with the taste of him. She opened her mouth then, letting him inside her, as their tongues met in a primal dance. She wanted him in every way, as she felt herself grow wet, the slickness in her thong warm as he put his hands on her hips and pulled her closer to him.

She felt him grow hard. Was that all him? Width and…all? Then, his hand reached down and unhooked her jeans. Right here? In the…elevator? She sucked in a breath, and then his hand went down the front of her waistband, all the way to her slickness. She moaned in his mouth, as his gentle fingers explored her, his palm cupped her through her open jeans and her hips moved, pushing her deeper into his hands.

She no longer cared about the elevator, or the cameras that might surely be here. Was some security officer somewhere watching him claim her? She couldn't care less. She almost felt like she could come right there. Then, the elevator dinged, and his hand slid out of her thong, releasing the smell of herself in the small space. He grinned at her, and pulled her down the empty, carpeted hallway to a corner room as she held her jeans together. He slipped the card into the door and it swung open, his lips once more finding hers as he backed her into the room. Once she broke free she had only a second to glance around at the huge suite: a master bedroom and separate living room, and windows with a spectacular view of the other skyscrapers along Chicago's lakefront. A single lamp was lit in the corner, giving off a golden light, and the crisp white linens on the bed were turned down, an offering to them both.

The door clicked shut behind them and now it was just her and Mr. X. It was then she realized she didn't really know his name, didn't know anything about him, and yet here she was, pants undone, alone with him in his hotel room, his fingers carrying her scent.

Could she really do this? He took off his own shirt, and she was amazed by his chest, chiseled with muscle. Her belly grew warmer. Then, he took a step toward her, wordlessly, and tugged at her sweater. She lifted her arms, unable to resist him and her top came off.

"I—I've never done this before…with a stranger, I mean," she murmured. He nibbled her nipple, the flick of teeth on the soft skin making her shiver. "This is… I mean, this is crazy. I don't usually do this."

He straightened. A lazy grin spread across his handsome face, warming up his squared off jaw. "Even good girls should be bad, once in a while."

She felt his hands on her jeans, gently tugging them downward. He walked her a step backward and she sat on the edge of the bed, her jeans around her knees. He knelt and pulled them off, as he took in her bare skin. He laid kisses on her bare legs.

She was a good girl. She never did this kind of thing.

"I just can't believe..." She wasn't even sure how she'd gotten here this fast, how she'd met a man and within an hour, was letting him see her everything. To put his hands and his mouth on her body. "I just... I don't know anything about you."

"You having second thoughts?" He paused, hazel eyes fixing her in a locked stare.

"No," she said. No, she wanted him. She did.

He pressed his hard, muscled chest against hers, dipping his face so close their noses nearly touched. "And all you need to know about me is this," he promised. She felt heat rise in her very core. He wanted her as much as she wanted him. And, God, did she want him. She'd wanted this the moment they'd met in the hotel bar an hour ago. She'd decided then in that split second to let him do what he wanted. She was willing.

"You can tell me whatever you want me to do to you. I want you to tell me."

She sucked in a breath and her knees trembled slightly. She didn't have to be a good girl. Not with him. She could be bad. Very, very bad. She could do whatever she wanted. She could let him do...whatever he wanted.

"Are you ready for the night of your life?" he growled in her ear, as he slipped his hand past the thin fabric of her lace thong, his fingers finding her soft center. "Well, well," he murmured, appreciative. "You're more than ready."

Then, he smiled at her, putting her at ease. He was so handsome, so warm. Did it matter what his name was? Or that she didn't know where he lived? Or…anything at all about him. He was a walking puzzle piece, and she wasn't sure where he fit. But the attraction between them was undeniable.

"You're beautiful," he said, as he pulled her closer to him, kissing her once more. She kissed him back, feeling the heat once more in her belly.

"So smooth," he said, as he grasped her knees, sliding his hands up the top of her thighs. Then he leaned over her and trailed a line of seductive kisses down the tops of her breasts making her shudder. He pressed his lips gently, almost reverently against her skin, as if worshipping every inch of her. She couldn't help it. She felt like a queen.

Then he moved backward, straightening. She leaned forward and touched his bare chest, so smooth, so…fit. He sucked in a breath as she leaned forward and gently laid a kiss between his brown nipples.

He groaned, throwing his own shirt to the ground while she explored the ridges of his abs. So tight, she thought, so… solid. He put his hands in her hair, and she glanced up at him. He knelt down, putting his hands on her knees once more.

"I'm going to make you come now." The promise sent

a thrill through her as the breath caught in her throat. He gently moved her knees apart, and she lay back on her elbows, his eyes never leaving hers. "I'm going to make you come again and again."

She believed him, as he laid a gentle kiss on the inside of her thigh. Then, suddenly, she knew what he intended. She wanted to tell him…wait… because going down…well, she felt self-conscious a little. What if she smelled? What if he didn't like how she tasted? And, Devin…well, Devin flat-out refused to do it.

He squeezed her inner thigh.

"I want to taste you," he said. "I want to worship you. Will you let me?"

His declaration sent a thrill through her. He didn't mind doing this. No, he *wanted* to do it. Worship her? Yes, please. She nodded, frozen by his determined gaze.

He moved upward, gently, teasing kisses leading a trail straight to her center. She arched her back, at once wanting and not wanting him to do what he promised—she suddenly felt self-conscious. Was her shower still good from earlier? Had the wax job she'd gotten still held? All those busy, insecure thoughts ran through her mind.

Then, he kissed her… there. Laid his lips on her most delicate part, his tongue flicking outward in a gentle exploration. The minute his tongue touched her, she felt white-hot molten heat roll through her.

"Oh," she moaned, her senses overtaken by his warmth. He held his tongue there, and the warm wetness overtook her. He was… He was good at this. She'd never had someone… so good at this. Instantly, she felt her arousal grow, her want for him. The desire built as he worked, teasing her at first, gently, with little flicks of his tongue.

He lifted his head a moment. "You taste so… amazing," he murmured. "God, Emma," he groaned as he pleasured her, lapping deeper into her center, devouring her. He slipped a finger inside her, tickling her, teasing her, caressing all those nerve endings inside. She'd never felt so wanted… so desired. Emma arched her back, moved into his hungry mouth and then suddenly she was on the edge of orgasm, every muscle in her body tensed. This never happened so quickly… Never… And then she was over the edge, consumed by Mr. X's talented tongue, her body rippling with pleasure as she cried out. The release took them both by surprise. She glanced down at him. This man whom she'd known just an hour, had just given her one of the best orgasms of her life.

"You sure are talented, Mr. X," she breathed, as her heart rate began to return to normal.

"Oh, you haven't seen anything yet," he promised. She felt her body come to life once more. Hungry again, as if this first climax was a simple appetizer, something to curb her appetite which only seemed to grow. He anticipated her every want, every need, and his gentle touch set her skin on fire.

Now it was her turn. She sat up, and grabbed his belt

loop, tugging him closer. She unzipped his pants and released him, closing her hands around him, amazed at his size. She'd never seen one so…big. She worked him with both hands as he leaned into her touch, letting out a small moan, and then she leaned over and put the tip of him in her mouth, teasing him with her tongue and he clutched at her shoulders, his entire body tensing and she knew she had him, knew she was driving him as crazy as he'd driven her. The power made her light-headed, and she felt even bolder. She worked him deeper and he ran his hand down her back. He pulled her up then and kissed her with an open mouth, his tongue urgently meeting hers in a primitive dance. She felt all her baser instincts take over. This was pure lust, amazing, animal lust. She'd never wanted a man so badly as in this moment.

He pulled away from her in that moment. "What do you want, Emma?"

She felt dazed, off-center. "I want you to fuck me." The words came out low, hoarse. She'd never said that out loud to anyone before.

A knowing smile played at the corners of his mouth, as he reached out and gave her nipple a teasing little pinch. It sent a shiver of delight through her. "Are you sure?"

She nodded, once, mouth open, her whole body feeling like one quivering nerve.

He reached for a condom from his discarded jeans

then and ripped the foil open easily. Then he was rolling it down his ample self, which stood ready to take her in the basest way possible.

CHAPTER SIX

For Xavier, every new woman was a gift, and yet, he couldn't remember feeling this kind of eagerness before. From the moment they met, he knew she'd be amazing, and here she was, beautifully naked in front of him, offering herself up in the most vulnerable way. He wanted her. Badly. He'd wanted her the moment he'd laid eyes on her at the bar, and now, here she was, giving herself to him. He'd always been a man to appreciate all kinds of women: short, tall, ample-chested, flat-chested, he enjoyed them all. But Emma was different somehow, just the best combination of curve and muscle, and her lean, lithe, perfectly proportioned body just screamed *playground.*

Her legs parted for him and he felt a ripple of desire as he teased her with just the head, running it around her wetness, as she lifted her pelvis up to meet him.

"Don't tease me," she cried, which made him want to tease her all the more, push her to the very edge of sanity. She spread her legs wider, willing him inside her, making him feel giddy. He pushed inside her a single centimeter and then withdrew.

"Oh!" she cried, grasping at him.

He teased her a bit further, maddeningly, as she clutched at his arms, frustration growing on her face.

"More," she cried, when he gave her just his full tip.

When she was almost at her wit's end, then he pushed into her tight center, a gasp escaping both their lips as he moved in on top of her, her warm, soft breasts pressing against him. He almost wanted to come right there, she felt so amazing. Was there anything better than this moment? This moment when he entered a woman for the first time? Xavier didn't know it.

"Is this what you wanted?" he murmured in her ear.

"Yes," she croaked, her voice dry. "Yes."

And he worked her harder, as her hips met his. He wanted to come at every moment. She was beyond delicious. Everything about her overwhelmed his senses. The smell of her. The taste of her. The feel of her. Xavier had been with many women in his life, and he appreciated them all, but Emma.... Emma just felt special. Not only was she gorgeous, but he'd never been with a woman so at odds with herself. In the bar, she'd been buttoned-up, conservative, even, he thought, on the verge of leaving, but once he'd gotten her into his hotel room, she'd turned into someone else: a woman overcome by desire and want, not caring about anything but satisfaction. Her passion ran deep, and the dichotomy thrilled him. He needed to have her in every way possible.

He withdrew, and turned her over so she was on her hands and knees in front of him, her amazing ass on display, her shell-pink lips exposed. He took her then from behind, enjoying her in the most primal of ways. He licked his finger then and reached around and touched her. She threw her head back and moaned, moving against him as he pushed deeper inside her. God, she was so tight. Amazingly tight. He feared he wouldn't be able to hold it, and then, she gave a hoarse shout as she came, tightening even more around him in spasms of pleasure. He grasped her hips then, thrusting slowly and deeply as she rode the waves of her climax. He loved making this woman come.

He withdrew and rolled her over, marveling at her flushed face. Her chest heaved as she tried to catch her breath. He dipped down and put a swollen pink nipple in his mouth. She groaned. He flicked his tongue, and she moaned again. He ran his teeth along her nipple and she shuddered beneath him. He went to the other nipple, running his teeth over the edge ever so softly.

"Oh, God," she murmured, her nipples standing at complete attention, as he nuzzled one breast. She watched him. "W-what is it that you'd want? To ask a stranger…"

Xavier smiled. There were so many things. So many things he'd asked women to do for him. But he knew exactly what he wanted her to do.

Xavier pulled her to the edge of the bed then, standing in front of her.

He entered her once more, this time with her flat on her back, knees up. She gasped as she took the full length of him.

"I want you to touch yourself," he said. "I want to watch you."

Emma hesitated ever so slightly, but then, as he watched, her hand snaked downward. Gently, she touched her self, delicately at first. Her eyes slid shut.

"No," he commanded. "Watch me, Emma. Watch me."

Her eyes flicked open and met his gaze. He saw her eyes widen as she brought herself closer to a third time, and he could feel her grow wetter. What he wanted was to watch her face as she came, that beautiful face. It was the most vulnerable a person could be, and he wanted to see it. Most women couldn't do it: most women looked away. Would Emma be able to hold eye contact?

He moved faster, deeper, never breaking eye contact. She held his, her blue eyes turning bluer as the redness crept up her cheek.

"That's it," he coaxed her. "Come for me."

Her blue eyes grew more urgent then with need, and as he thrust deeper, suddenly, her whole body tensed. Her toes curled beside him, and then, eyes never leaving his, she dissolved, the climax taking her past the edge, tumbling her into oblivion. Her eyes turned a brilliant blue as they held his, the most beautiful thing he'd ever seen in his life: the raw vulnerability of this beautiful woman as she came. Then, instantly, he poured himself inside her in a rush of nearly unbearable pleasure. She'd pulled it out of him, demanded it, and he'd given it to her.

They didn't get much sleep. Xavier didn't sleep at all, truth be told. He held this beautiful woman in his arms, cradling her naked against him beneath the thin cotton sheet of the hotel bed. He breathed in her scent: hints of earthiness and the fresh, bright smell of lavender shampoo in her hair. They'd ended the night in the shower, where he'd gently washed every amazing curve, the suds slipping down her taut body in all the right places. He'd worked up the lather, but she'd been the one to turn the tables on him. She'd gotten on her knees and taken him in her mouth, making him come one last mind-blowing time. Before that, they'd gone twice more that evening, trying out almost every position he could think of, as he worked hard to sate his growing desire for her. Normally, by now in a *Nost* tryst, he'd tire, begin to have his fill, start planning his getaway, but Emma was different. Every time she climaxed, every time she brought him over the edge, she seemed to grow more beautiful. Every time they joined together, the experience felt brand new, his exploration of her seemed never to grow dull. They fit together in a way that took him by surprise. They moved together like a couple who'd known each other for years: she seemed to anticipate his every want. Even now, as she lay sleeping against him, he felt his groin stirring. A full night and usually he was spent, drained, done for, but his body *still* wanted her in the most animalistic way. Was this what it meant to be a slave to passion?

Or…a slave to love?

Suddenly, he remembered something his father had told him: *No man can resist the woman he loves.* He shook the thought from his head. He hadn't thought about his father—or his troubled mother—for years. Why now?

Was it Emma? Had she somehow dredged up memories he thought long buried?

Was this more than sex? It felt like…more.

Emma just gave all of herself. Even now, as she slept pressed against him, she held nothing back. Most women were careful. Most women kept a part of themselves hidden away from him. Most women… No, nearly all women, couldn't look him in the eye when they came—perhaps too embarrassed, or too unwilling to show just how vulnerable they could be. Emma let herself be seen. She'd been so open and honest, she'd laid herself completely bare, and, somehow, that got to him. She'd given him a gift, a precious gift.

So that meant he'd fall in love?

He pressed his eyes shut. He wasn't going to fall for this woman. He couldn't. He thought of Sasha, of her dark, penetrating eyes and the curves that didn't quit. He'd been a slave to her, and she'd crushed his heart. Left him broken and helpless. He still remembered the gut-punch he'd felt the day he'd discovered the text messages, the half-naked pictures she'd sent to another man, the declaration of how she couldn't wait to have him inside her. Sasha had lived a double life, and the worst part was that he'd failed her. He'd failed to satisfy her. She'd gone elsewhere, looking for the pleasure he apparently couldn't give her. He'd known that their sex life had become a bit stale. He thought it was what naturally happened in a long-term relationship. They'd become too used to each other, too familiar, and he hadn't known they had to break out of that.

Sasha had…by seeking attention elsewhere.

The memories still hurt, like little razor blades through his mind. He wasn't even sure he *could* love another woman again, could leave himself so open to hurt. He'd built an emotional wall so thick and tall, he wasn't even sure how to get through it anymore. *Yet, she had,* a voice whispered in his mind. *She's made a crack in that wall.*

No. He'd have to fortify it again.

She murmured and snuggled into him, and his body responded as he cradled her against him. He wasn't sure he wanted this to end. Wasn't sure he wanted to say goodbye to her.

In another twelve hours, her profile will be hidden from me, a small, urgent voice told him. *But then, the decision will be made for me,* he thought. He felt both a smidgen of relief and a stab of panic but decided that it would be best to let the app take care of this for him. If he saw too much more of her, he would fall for her. Of this, he was certain, and then what? He knew what happened to all long-term relationships: the sex died, the desire died, and then came betrayal and heartbreak. It just wasn't feasible to keep the passion alive. He thought of Sasha. At this point, could he really blame her? She'd cheated first, but wouldn't he have eventually? Human beings need passion.

And there was nothing more passionate than sex with a stranger. Why ruin the amazing night they'd had by letting it get boring…predictable?

Xavier's phone jangled on the bedside table, announcing the alarm he'd set just two hours ago. He had a meeting at *Nost* to discuss new directions of the app, which member roll was growing bigger every day. He had to get to work. Emma shifted against him, rubbing her full breasts against his side. The feel of her soft nipples against his skin sent a ripple of tightness through his groin. He wanted her again…yet, he had no time. As it was, he might be late. He dropped a kiss on the top of her head and she murmured, sweetly, still sleepy. He slipped from the covers to get dressed.

As he moved quickly and quietly, he watched this beautiful creature in his bed, her golden hair spilled out over the pillow, her pink lips parted as she slept. The white curve of her shoulder just visible beneath the edge of the sheet. She lay deliciously naked beneath it, her skin almost calling to him. He wanted nothing more than to climb back into bed with her and taste her all over again. He wanted to feel her again, explore the very depths of her. See if they were as amazing on the repeat as they were the first time. But he couldn't. His phone vibrated with incoming messages from his partner at *Nost.* He needed to get in the office.

He bent down and laid a gentle kiss on Emma's temple. She shifted but she fought with sleep, as it tugged her deeper downward. He wanted to stay here, watch her sleep, memorize every detail of her face. He wanted to keep this with him, this amazing night. He half wished she'd wake, but as he touched her golden hair, she dug in with a satisfied murmur. Even now, she was vulnerable and trusting: sleeping so deeply with him, a stranger. Emma simply didn't hold back. She put herself in his hands.

He felt the need to care for her. He reached down and pulled up the warmer blanket, tucking it over her bare shoulder. She let out a satisfied sigh. God, she was perfect.

Now's the time to leave, he thought. *When she's still perfect.*

Reluctantly, he turned to leave, grabbing his wallet and cell phone. On his way out, he saw the hotel pad and pen on the desk. On a whim, he scribbled a quick note and then smiled to himself.

They technically still had twelve hours on the *Nost*

clock, he reminded himself. A lot could be done in twelve hours.

He opened the hotel room door and slipped out, careful to make sure the door shut quietly behind him.

CHAPTER SEVEN

A BURST OF chimes from her phone woke Emma with a start. The hotel room was dark, the light-canceling shades drawn, and for a second she was disoriented. Where was she? Then she realized she was naked beneath expensive thick cotton sheets. *Mr. X.* Memories of the night before flooded her mind and all the various ways they'd explored each other's bodies. Her neck grew hot just thinking of his strong hands on her body. That was by far the most amazing sex she'd ever had. Bar none. She sat up in bed and found it empty.

Where was he? The bathroom light was on, door ajar. She opened her mouth to call his name, but then remembered with shocking clarity that she didn't know it. Was she really going to shout out, "Mr. X?" to the room?

Oh, God. Had she really done this? Had she really fucked the brains out of a man and she *didn't even know his name*?

Sure, she knew women did this all the time. Sarah came to mind. This was probably her normal Tuesday night.

But Emma? Never. As in, not once. Not at a frat party, or a club, or a bar. She'd never taken a stranger into her bed. She thought of all the many ways they'd gotten to know each other last night. Not so strange anymore, she realized. Emma could practically sketch his amazingly fit body in her mind. She might not know his name, but she sure knew every other thing about him.

She studied the light from the bathroom. "Hello?" she called from the bed. No answer. Emma pulled the top sheet off the bed and padded over to the bathroom, finding it empty.

"Huh," she murmured out loud as she crossed the room to the curtained window. She flung back the curtain and sunlight poured in. Outside, the day had already begun, and far below the street was crowded with small cars and the sidewalks teemed with people on their way to work. The Loop bustled with energy and focus. She'd soon be among the throng, making her way to the L. She glanced at her phone. She had a half hour to shower and get dressed, then she'd need to head home and finish up that last article that her editor wanted today. Such was the life of a freelancer.

Emma turned, and that was when she saw the letter on the nightstand. She went to it, reading the precise, neat handwriting:

8 p.m. tonight. Meet you in the lobby.

A little thrill ran through her. He wanted to see her again? Was this something that happened with *Nost*? She thought it was purely for one-night stands. But there was also no mistaking what Mr. X wanted. He wanted more sex. Tonight. *Here.*

She could feel a little tingle in her inner thigh. Yes, please. More of him, please.

Then she felt deliciously naughty. *I don't know the man's name. Nothing. And I'm coming back for more.*

She folded the note carefully and tucked it into her bag. Then, she bit her bottom lip. She really *ought* to know his name. Some detail about him. She searched her brain, but came up with nothing. He'd vaguely said something the night before about working in tech, but that could mean anything. She had no idea where he lived or worked. She did know that he came alive beneath her touch, that he loved it when she focused her tongue on the tip of his…

Suddenly, the room got hotter. Emma absently cupped her own breast through the sheet, remembering Mr. X doing the same thing the night before, remembering the feel of his teeth against her nipple. She felt a rush of heat then, and almost felt the urge to slip her hands beneath the sheet and touch herself.

She shook her head. What was happening to her? Just thinking of Mr. X sent her into a tailspin. She glanced at her phone. Emma needed to get ready. She retreated to the bathroom to find the shower where just hours ago, Mr. X had sudsed her down, washing every part of her in delicate, perfect circles. She turned on the pizza pan–sized shower head, and the room soon filled with steam. Mr. X was everywhere in this room, and her body felt like he'd claimed it. As she let the sheet fall down, she remembered everywhere he'd touched her, every little ripple of pleasure he'd sent through her body. Suddenly, it seemed that the evening felt like years away. She wasn't sure she could wait.

Xavier arrived at his corner office in the west Loop in a four-story brownstone not far from the United Center. Inside, the building was all gleaming new tech company: open floor plan, stocked fridge, ping-pong table in the glassed conference room that sat in the middle of the office space on the raised first floor. The open floor plan accommodated just four offices: one for each of *Nost*'s partners. Everyone else worked in glassed-in cubes. As it was a pet-friendly office, dogs sat near various cubes, and a big bowl of dog treats was laid at the front desk. Xavier wanted to push for in-office day care, but so far, only two employees had children, not enough to make a program.

The staff of *Nost* was almost all young, hip and attractive. It hadn't been on purpose, but the people who'd showed up for the job interviews just fit that bill. Pets were their priority, and kids seemed a long way off. It made sense to Xavier. Not too many forty-somethings with families would be looking to work for a hookup dating site.

Xavier crossed the main office floor just in time to get the knowing look from his assistant, Justin Tanaka. Justin wore his usual uniform of colored bow tie, slate-gray vest and skinny jeans. The color of the vest and bow tie changed daily, but the general outfit did not. He wore wingtips on his feet and his thick, jet-black hair in a precise cut.

"Well, well, *well,*" Justin crooned as Xavier arrived, hopping up from his desk and following Xavier into his office. "Wearing the same clothes from yesterday?"

"Only you would notice that," Xavier grumbled as he put down his messenger bag. Justin, just twenty-four, was the best personal assistant: on time, organized, a hard worker. His only flaw was his nosiness, but Xavier didn't mind. Justin kept things lively, and he was instrumental in making sure *Nost* was LGBT friendly.

"Of course I would." Justin rolled his eyes and put a hand on his hip, jutting it out for emphasis.

Xavier laughed. "I know. You don't let the office forget it."

"Hey, if you've got it, flaunt it." Justin shrugged one shoulder, back to his normal, less theatrical self. "So..." Justin perched himself on Xavier's desk. "Tell me...who was the lucky *Nost* girl?"

"Emma," Xavier said, sitting at his computer and pulling up his email.

"Emma! I like that name. My cousin's named Emma. Let's see, that makes..." Justin mimed flipping through a binder. "Girl number 438."

"There haven't been that many," Xavier protested, glancing up from his keyboard.

"Oh, my bad. That's 437. Better watch out or you'll break my record."

Xavier eyed him. "Which is?"

Justin quirked an eyebrow. "You don't want to know."

Xavier laughed. "You're right. I *don't* want to know."

Justin crossed his arms across his vest. "All right, mister. Remember you've got the meeting with the board at eleven, and this evening, the development team wanted to know if you'd join them for their happy hour at seven."

"Can't do it," Xavier said, categorically, thinking about Emma and the lobby of the Ritz-Carlton. "I've got plans."

Justin quirked an eyebrow. "With Emma?" Xavier said nothing, but something in his face must've given the truth away, because Justin shrieked, "You are! You're going out with Emma *two* nights in a row?" He clicked his tongue to the roof of his mouth with disapproval. "You're dipping your wick in the same well! What will this do to our brand?!"

"Technically, *Nost* promotes the forty-eight-hour relationship," Xavier explained, as he typed in his email password. "And it hasn't been forty-eight hours yet."

Justin narrowed his eyes, doubtful. "Mmm-hmm. You sure you're not developing a thing for this girl?"

Xavier laughed. "No," he said, shaking his head. "You know I don't do that. It's the whole reason I founded this company."

The company his father told him was a mistake.

"Love needs more than forty-eight hours," he told his son a year ago, before the last heart attack took him.

"Papi, this isn't about love," he told his father, who'd simply arched an eyebrow and replied, "Isn't everything about love?"

The damn romantic. More and more, memories of his father kept popping up lately. He wondered why. It had been a year since Xavier had put him in the ground at the graveyard next to his mother. A year he'd been an orphan, and he'd done pretty well by himself: had launched a wildly successful company. Had found comfort in the arms of many women… Maybe not 437. But a sizable number.

"There's a first time for everything." Justin's dark eyes gleamed. "You know the *only* constant in this world is change."

"Does that come with a free side of zen meditation?"

"If you'd like. Want me to pencil that in for you?"

Xavier laughed. "No thanks." He didn't need meditation or yoga. He just needed to see Emma one last time.

Justin gave him a knowing look as if he could read his mind. "Well, I'll leave you to it. And remember, no texting this girl Emma. You didn't get her phone number, did you?"

"No," Xavier replied.

"Good. Maybe there's hope for you, after all." Justin sauntered back to his desk.

Was there? Xavier wondered. Was he developing a thing for Emma? No, he told himself. Just one more night. One more night to scratch this little itch. One more night ought to do it. He'd never gone three nights before, never found a need to go beyond the forty-eight-hour rule. But, he admitted, he'd hardly ever come back for seconds either. Usually one night was plenty. One night and he'd felt satiated. But not with Emma. What made her different? He'd need to see her again to find out.

He pushed the little worry out of his brain. It didn't mean he was falling in love with her, did it? The sex was amazing, more than amazing, sizzling hot, but that didn't mean he needed to go pick out wedding bands. Plus, if he really wanted to cool things off, he ought to just start dating her. Propose. Like he did with Sasha. That would fix his want and hers—for good. They'd be a bored couple in no time.

He sat at his desk and logged in to his computer, pulling up the code for *Nost.* It was brilliantly simple, and yet teasingly complex. He loved it. It had been his baby and he still liked to tweak it. He remembered Happy Fun Time from last night and frowned. The man had violated pretty much *every Nost* behavior guideline at the bar last night. He pulled up the man's profile. Whose pictures was he using? Not his own. Xavier squinted. No way that male model was the same man he'd seen in the Cardinals hat the night before. And the little *c* and *v* next to his name…might not even be his real name. He might not be vetted at all. He remembered the way the man had talked to Emma the night before and his blood boiled just thinking about it.

With a few keystrokes, he turned up the Facebook profile, where Xavier saw the real Happy Fun Time clearly had stolen his pictures. He'd stolen this man's identity, whoever he was, and was using it as a front on *Nost.*

Xavier clacked away on the keyboard and with a few commands, barred Happy Fun Time from the app. For good. Still, uneasiness lingered. The guy used a name that wasn't his, and he could do it again. He could slip into the roster of *Nost* under another stolen name at a later date. The thought irked Xavier. He wanted the app to be safe and to be fun, and it would be neither if assholes like Happy Fun Time found ways around *Nost*'s safety settings.

Xavier made a mental note to ask the security guys for a way around this. He worried Happy Fun Time wasn't the only one gaming the system. Still, he'd have to have the man's social security number in order to run the verified test. But plenty of identity thieves had numbers that weren't theirs. Xavier shot an email to his friend, a Chicago police detective, asking his advice.

Xavier focused on his computer once more. He had the information of every *Nost* user at his fingertips. Yes, the site was publicly anonymous, but on the back end, there was all kinds of personal information he could find. Names, addresses, phone numbers.

His fingers paused on his keyboard. Should he look up Emma's information?

He glanced outward through his walls of his glassed-in office at Justin's back as he worked. He shouldn't, he knew. It violated tons of ethics standards, but…

No. Xavier closed the window on his machine.

I shouldn't do it. Should I?

He tried to focus on work emails, but he kept being drawn back to the minimized box on his computer screen. The *Nost* app database.

Eventually, he could resist no more. The temptation was just too great. What could it really hurt?

With a few clicks of the mouse, he'd pulled up Emma's information. Emma Allaire, age twenty-eight, lived in Lincoln Square. Before he could stop himself, he'd searched her on social media, and found her Instagram account. Dozens of pictures rolled up for him, as she had her account public. As he scrolled through them: her with her friends, her with what looked like her mom, several of Emma at her favorite coffee shop on North Avenue… He felt a surge of guilt. He was snooping, stalking even. And what was he even doing? Not only was he invading her privacy, but he was doing the very thing he told himself would kill their attraction: he was trying to get to know her.

Yet, he gobbled up every new bit of information like a starving man. He'd never felt this way about any *Nost* girl before. After exploring their bodies, he'd been content to just let them go. But something about Emma was different. She intrigued him.

Was it her fire? Her determination to challenge him on his beliefs that a no-strings relationship was the best kind? Was it the way she'd stood up to Happy Fun Time at the bar? Or, was it the way she'd given herself to him so authentically, so honestly the night before. She'd let herself be vulnerable in a way no woman had before, not even Sasha.

He soon found her articles online and devoured them, one after another. Emma came across as thoughtful, razor-sharp and insightful. More liberal than he on most issues, he found, she was the kind of woman who wasn't afraid to put herself out there. To let others know how she really felt. Her writing mimicked her passion the night before. Emma was just herself—no pretense.

He found that amazingly refreshing.

So many of the women he'd been with were so concerned with pleasing him, with molding themselves into something they thought he'd like, rather than just being *them.* He made no apologies for who he was and always wanted a partner do the same.

Before he'd realized what he was doing, he'd spent the entire morning combing the internet for information on Emma.

But, he reasoned, it didn't mean anything. Did it?

CHAPTER EIGHT

Emma threw on a sweater and headed out of her modest, one-bedroom Lincoln Square condo. She skipped down two flights and outside into the fresh fall air. The morning chill had lifted beneath the bright, warm haze of the midday sun, and the leaves on the trees were beginning to turn shades of red and gold. A cab rushed down her tree-lined street as she made her way for Armitage Street nearby. She wasn't sure if it was the beautiful fall day in the city or the fact she still felt like she was glowing from her amazing night with Mr. X, but everything just felt shinier...and brighter.

Emma turned the corner and saw the little diner where she'd planned to meet Sarah for lunch. She saw her pretty redheaded friend sitting at a booth near the window and waved to her as she slipped inside and almost skipped to the booth where Sarah sat. Sarah, wearing one of her striking business suits, stood and gave her friend a hug.

"You got laid," Sarah declared, the second Emma sat down.

"What? How do you know that?" Emma exclaimed.

"Because you're *literally* glowing. Radioactive glowing. So... Happy Fun Time was...happy?" Sarah sat, adjusting her expensive wool blazer. No doubt, she planned an afternoon of showing off business offices to corporate representatives.

Emma wrinkled her nose. "God no. He was horrible. Probably a date rapist. Maybe a serial killer."

"Oh, no." Sarah leaned forward. "Then don't tell me you hooked up with your ex, because so help me..." Sarah was no fan of Devin's. She'd once said he was about as exciting as watching someone else watch paint dry.

"No! He's in Seattle." Emma shook her head furiously even as the waitress sat down waters in front of them and a couple of laminated menus. "No, another *Nost* candidate. Mr. X."

"Ooh. Mr. X. Mysterious. I like it. Have a picture?" Emma pulled up Mr. X's profile on her phone and showed her friend. Sarah snatched the phone out of Emma's hand.

"No way." She peered at Mr. X's photograph. "I'm impressed." Sarah bit her pink lip. "Now, this is what I'm talking about." She handed Emma's phone back. "Now...on to a new one tonight?" she half joked as she picked up the menu.

"New one! No. I'm going to meet Mr. X again."

Sarah dropped the menu in her hands. "Emma. *No*

Strings. No second dates!" Sarah shook her head. "Second dates just get…complicated."

Emma felt a little disappointment. "Why?"

Sarah shook her head. "Because. Then, you start to almost expect to see them. Best to just keep it at a single date. Trust me. Guys are the worst. You think they'll be able to cut things off easier than women, but sometimes, it's just the opposite."

"What do you mean?" The waitress returned and quickly took their orders. Sarah opted for a lightly dressed salad, and Emma, feeling famished from all her exercise the night before, chose a hamburger and fries.

"Just that. Last time I went on a second date, the guy online stalked me. Started leaving messages for me on Facebook. I had to eventually block him." Sarah took a sip of water and shrugged. "He actually said he wanted to marry me!"

"No way!" Emma shook her head. "I mean…what on earth did you do to him?"

"What didn't I do?" Sarah shrugged and laughed a little at her own joke. Her green eyes sparkled with mischief. "But he just couldn't keep up with me. He was just too vanilla. Sweet, but there's no way I would've wanted a long-term relationship with him."

"Well, I don't mind if Mr. X turns into…more." Emma thought of Mr. X's strong hands, his sexy hazel eyes, the way he seemed to *know* her, even though they hadn't known each other that long. She wouldn't mind that turning into a regular thing.

"No!" Sarah slapped her hand on the table. "Emma. We talked about this. You are just too quick to settle. That's what happened with Devin, remember?"

Emma nodded, reluctantly. "But Mr. X is *nothing* like Devin. They're polar opposites."

"From the picture you showed me, I believe that much is true, but still. The whole point of this little exercise is to show you how many fish there are in the sea."

The waitress appeared then with their lunches, setting the plates in front of the women. Emma dug into her fries like a woman who hadn't seen food in days.

Sarah quirked an eyebrow. "Well, I can see Mr. X worked up an appetite in you." Emma coughed.

"You have no idea," she said, between mouthfuls.

"Well, then. Tell me. All the juicy bits!" Sarah leaned in, eager.

Later that afternoon, Emma sat at her computer and stared at the cursor. What on earth was she going to write? Nearly all of her date with Mr. X was…uh, X-rated. At least, the good parts were. She couldn't imagine how her editor would even *go* for something so…graphic. After all, their online magazine was read mostly by working moms, not co-eds looking for the *hottest tips for spicing up the old blowjob.* She glanced at the handwritten note from Mr. X and felt a little shiver of anticipation. She'd see him again tonight.

She didn't even know his name!

All the things he'd done to her and she had no idea what his first name was. More than anything, she wanted to find out. Yet, as she pulled up Google to start her search, she had no idea how to start. "Amazing hazel eyes and abs that won't quit… Chicago?"

"Mr. X Chicago?"

Both of those searches pulled up beefcake photos and one news article about a TV pilot being shot in downtown.

Argh. She searched *Nost and Mr. X*, but just got his profile, which she realized with a start as she looked at the little wristwatch graphic in the corner, would disappear from her feed sometime this evening. A little prick of panic tickled the back of her neck. What if she never got his name? What if she never saw him again after tonight?

But there would be tonight, and then…she'd just ask him. Flat out. What's your name? Can I have your number?

Because I want to fuck you many, many more times.

The naughty thought popped into her head unbidden, shocking her. She sat for a few minutes, staring at the blinking cursor, but all she could think about was Mr. X's golden eyes on her while she came for him, the way he'd held her, as if keeping her under his spell. She'd never felt so exposed, yet, so protected at the same time.

Maybe it was the thrill of being with a stranger. She could do things she never dared with someone she knew.

Emma knew she'd get no work done today. She opted instead to try to find an outfit for tonight. She rummaged through her drawers, but even the laciest of her lingerie seemed not sexy enough. She grabbed her bag and decided to head to the stores on Armitage. She was going to stop at the lingerie shop.

Emma stood anxiously in the lobby of the Ritz-Carlton, wondering if she'd arrived too early. It was ten until eight, ten full minutes before Mr. X had set the meeting date. The lobby was mostly empty, with just a couple of workers behind the desk and few patrons milling about. The elevators dinged occasionally, announcing the arrival of a new guest, and Emma found it hard not to glare at each one, hoping to see Mr. X's face. She wore a tight black dress, one she hadn't worn in years. It was stretchy and long-sleeved, and clung to her curves. Beneath the dress, she wore the most delicate laced thong she'd ever owned, a matching push-up bra, and actual thigh-high lacy tights, which she'd never worn her whole life. But the idea of Mr. X peeling them off her had made them a must-buy. She wore stiletto heels and carried a small clutch bag. She'd tied her blond hair up this time in a messy bun, with silver dangling earrings that skimmed her jawline when she moved her head. She felt…pretty. She also felt…very much like she wanted to get back up to that hotel room with Mr. X.

Her stomach fluttered with nerves. She'd never before shown up at a hotel lobby with the express intent of sex. She felt beyond naughty. She was being bad, wasn't she? Good girls didn't do this. A flutter of nerves cinched her stomach. A bellboy went by with a golden cart full of bags, maneuvering around the giant fountain; he nodded at her, an appreciative look on his face.

But all she wanted was Mr. X.

Okay, she told herself, *just breathe. When he comes in, ask for his name and his number first. Then...*

She felt someone looking at her and at that moment glanced up to see Mr. X walking toward her from the other side of the lobby, beyond the fountain. Their eyes locked and she froze. He looked amazing, even taller than she remembered, even more darkly handsome than his *Nost* photo. His jet-black hair was perfectly combed. He smiled slightly as he saw her, a knowing smile. She felt a shiver run down her spine. It was as if he could see straight through her dress, straight to her sexy new lingerie, and the fact that she was already feeling a slickness between her legs. Just looking at the man made her wet.

He wore a button-down shirt and a leather jacket that only made his shoulders look broader. He covered the distance between them in no time.

"You look amazing," he told her, hazel eyes bright as he took a long sweep of her outfit.

"I hoped you'd like it," she said, feeling suddenly self-conscious.

"Oh, I do," he said, slipping his hand around the back of her waist. She moved into him and he kissed her, lightly. She deepened the kiss, lacing her hands around the back of his neck. He tasted like cinnamon: gum he must've been chewing. His hands wandered down the back of her dress, his hands squeezing her hips and running down the length of her.

When they finally broke apart, Emma's heart thudded in her chest. The fire between them was unmistakable, the attraction palpable. Emma no longer cared about the bellhops, or the hotel workers behind the desk.

"I want you," Mr. X murmured, so softly only she could hear. She nodded slowly.

"I want you, too." Emma hesitated. "But…first… what's your name?"

Mr. X grinned. "You know my name."

"Mr. X isn't your full name."

Mr. X considered her. "You want to know my name?" She nodded once more. "Then, you have to do something for me."

Emma felt the nerves tighten in her stomach. "Yes?"

Mr. X chuckled, a deep growl in his throat. She bit her bottom lip, waiting. He glanced around the lobby and then leaned in, his lips near her ear. "See that bathroom over there? Why don't you go in. Slip out of that sexy underwear you're wearing and bring it back to me."

Emma's head shot from side to side, as she glanced around the lobby, her face growing hot at the mere suggestion. But suddenly she wanted to do it. She liked the idea, even. Him telling her what to do. Her doing it. Something felt naughty about it. Naughty but right.

"All right." She accepted the challenge with a nod. She walked to the restroom, giving a quick glance over her shoulder. Mr. X leaned on the bar, watching every movement she made. She felt exhilarated then: he wanted her, just as much as she wanted him.

She pushed open the bathroom door to find one of the nicest bathrooms she'd ever seen: marble white countertops and gleaming floors. Real towels instead of paper ones, heavy oak doors that went all the way to the floor. The bathroom was empty and she slipped into the first stall. Her heart thudded in her chest as she raised the hem of her black dress. What was she doing? Was she really going to hand him her underwear? But then, she thought of the glint in his golden eyes, the spark of a challenge. She felt empowered suddenly as she whipped her thin, black lace thong off. Then she heard the bathroom door open and shoes clacking on the tile floor.

A soft knock came on her door. She jumped, startled.

"Ready for me?" Mr. X's smooth voice asked from the other side of the stall door. She whipped it open, shocked.

"What are you…" She didn't get to finish, before he'd swept in and was kissing her passionately, his hands on the hem of her dress. He yanked it upwards, revealing her bareness and her thigh-highs. He whistled, low.

"You are so fucking sexy," he murmured, as he leaned in and touched her, his fingers slipping into her wetness. She moaned and so did he as he worked her most tender spot. He bent down and kissed her, slipping his tongue into her mouth as his expert fingers brought her to the brink. She couldn't believe this was happening—a bathroom? The thought flittered across her mind. She'd never in a million years thought of having sex here…but now, with Mr. X's hands on her, all rational thought disappeared.

He flipped her around then in the oversized stall so that her hands were up on the wall, her dress pushed up to her waist, her legs trembling and inner thighs slick with wet. She heard him unzip, and the condom package rip open and then he was taking her from behind, filling her up with every inch of himself, and she gasped, louder than she intended, as her hands pressed against the slick tiled wall.

"I want you to come for me," he growled in her ear.

"I…" Could she? Her whole body felt like it was on fire, her whole self wanted him in a way she'd never wanted anyone.

"I want you to touch yourself," he commanded, in a voice that left no room for argument. She was hyper-aware that at any moment, someone could walk in, someone could hear them.

"Touch yourself," he demanded again, and then she did, her hand snaking downward, finding her sweet center. This was what she wanted. Pure, unadulterated lust, taken by a man who couldn't wait to get her in a bed. Couldn't wait to even get her fully undressed.

She pushed against her own hand, as he delved deeper and harder in her. She could feel the tension build. Oh, God, could she. Not caring about who might come in or who might hear them, she let go, toppling over the edge in a furious, urgent climax. She let out a shout, even as he, too, came inside her with a hard thrust. He collapsed against her, breathing hard.

"You are…so fucking perfect," he growled in her ear, as if even he couldn't believe it. "What are you doing to me?"

Her legs felt like jelly, and she didn't even know if she could move just yet. He withdrew, discarded the condom and zipped up, then kissed her neck as she pulled down the hem of her skirt. One thigh-high was now down around her knee.

"I'll keep these," he promised, tucking her G-string in his pocket. Then, he kissed the back of her neck once more.

"You promised your name," she said.

"Xavier," he said and slipped out of the stall.

"Xavier… What?" she asked, staying behind to straighten out her thigh-highs. She'd never had such an amazing orgasm so fast in a public space before. She felt light-headed and overcome, her knees literally wobbled as she stood up. The storm of passion had left her spent and panting, unsure of what to do next. Her head spun. The last time she'd even done anything so… public was in her college dorm study lounge.

"Xavier?" she called once more, but heard no response. She came out of the stall to find the restroom empty. Was he outside? She smoothed her now mussed hair as she rushed out.

The lobby, however, was empty.

Xavier was nowhere to be found.

CHAPTER NINE

XAVIER JUMPED INTO a waiting cab as his heart beat rapidly in his chest. He could still smell her on him, on his clothes, and his veins still buzzed with arousal and yearning for her. She ought to be in his arms right now. Hell, he ought to have taken her upstairs to a new room and taken her eight more times. But he couldn't. He was getting pulled in, as if Emma were quicksand. He'd felt that urge for more grow in him just when he thought it ought to be abating. He wanted to spend the night with her again and wake up with her in his arms, and he couldn't do that. He knew what it would mean if he did. He was falling for this girl. As he came he'd almost said, *I love you.*

Never before had he felt such swift emotions, not during sex, and certainly not with what amounted to a stranger. The last time he'd felt so consumed had been Sasha. And he had no intention of making that mistake again.

Leaving her now was the best thing he could do for them both. He'd thought that he could get her out of his system by having one last night with her, but now, he realized, she was like a highly addictive drug: the more times he went back, the more he'd need her. And he couldn't do that. He wasn't ready. Sasha had torn out his heart and he vowed never to let another woman get that close to him again.

His phone pinged, the *Nost* app alerting him to the fact that her profile was officially disappearing from his app in less than fifteen minutes. There was nothing he could do to prolong the inevitable. He'd been the one to engineer it, after all, and despite his partners wanting a fail-safe, a way of extending time, he'd been bullheaded about that feature.

"Can't close the deal in forty-eight? Then you start over," he'd said. And eventually he'd gotten everyone to agree with him. "You want a longer relationship than that? Then head to Bumble."

The board had eventually agreed. They couldn't be the "looking for love" app when they were strictly about no-strings. It was the way to set themselves apart in an already crowded market. But now, Xavier doubted himself. Had he done the right thing?

Still, he had her number. He had a way to contact her. He knew where she worked.

Can't do it, he told himself. *The sex was amazing, but that's all it was.* The words rang hollow even in his own head. He knew he was lying to himself, and yet, he stubbornly refused to admit it.

Instead, he decided to hit the gym. That's where he

went to work out his frustrations and maybe after an hour or two lifting weights his mind would be clearer and he'd get his mind off Emma's gorgeous, lean body and the way she gave herself so freely, came so deeply. He'd never had a woman offer up so much of herself to him so willingly, and he wondered if that included her heart as well. Would she love him as passionately as she fucked him? Thoughts of love unnerved him. What was he doing? He'd decided long ago that love was toxic. Why would he want that now?

He felt the urge to pull up Emma's Facebook, but then stopped himself. What was he doing? Becoming some creepy tech stalker? No. He needed to pull himself together. Emma was amazing, and their time together had been outstanding. But the *Nost* clock had less than one minute left.

Then, a message lit up his screen.

Where are you? she wrote to him on *Nost*. I...

Then, the app reset, her profile disappeared and the rest of the message was lost.

Emma watched her phone reconfigure *Nost*. Mr. X was suddenly gone from the app, and there was no way to find him, no way to continue the message.

"Damn it," she cursed as she sank into a leather couch near the fountain in the hotel lobby. What was she supposed to do now? She'd searched the bar, the lobby, and had even walked out to the street, but had found no sign of Mr. X. Xavier. That's all she knew about the man. She had no idea where he lived, how old he was, or what he did for a living other than the vague "work in the tech sector" explanation he'd given her.

Emma could feel a delicious soreness creeping in between her legs. Just moments ago Xavier had filled her up in the most intimate way possible, and now he was gone forever, a ghost, a stranger she might never see again. She couldn't understand why he'd left so quickly, why he'd bolted. Had she offended him in some way? Had she done something wrong?

Why had he left in such a hurry? She needed to know. She wanted to know. She had to see him again.

Maybe he was a wanted man, she wondered. It would explain a lot, and yet, Emma wouldn't believe Xavier was a felon. He'd told her about his fiancée betraying him and breaking his heart, but she'd never met a man so clearly petrified of commitment. She'd heard of toxic bachelors, but this was ridiculous. Emma glanced up at the lobby desk manned by a hotel clerk, a young man in his twenties. Emma got up and walked toward him. Maybe she could get answers.

"Hello." The clerk greeted her with a friendly smile. "May I help you, miss?"

"I was wondering if you could tell me if Xavier booked a room tonight. He had one last night. We were in room…" Emma stopped. What room were they in? 12…something. 1209? 1208? She racked her brain. She knew it was the twelfth floor, but why couldn't she remember? Granted, she'd been a little busy when Xavier had swept her inside to notice much about the golden numbers on the door. He'd had his mouth on hers, a memory that made her shiver with delight remembering his soft, determined tongue as it gently probed her. She felt her face flush. "Uh, a big suite. On the 12th floor. Maybe 1209?"

The clerk now studied her with suspicion. "There are *several* suites on the twelfth floor. Your name, miss?"

"Uh, Emma Allaire. But the room wasn't in my name. It was under Xavier's."

"Xavier…?" The clerk paused, waiting for the last name. But Emma didn't know it. That's what she needed to find out.

"Yes, Xavier."

"Xavier…*what*? His last name, please?"

Emma bit her lip. She realized she was going to get zero information from this clerk. She was sure this hotel had all kinds of privacy rules, and now that she thought about it, it was probably insane to just go asking about hotel guests. Besides, what was she supposed to tell this man? She'd had sex *multiple* times with a man and she didn't even know his last name? In fact, she could still feel the wetness of her own come between her legs from him taking in her their very restroom just a hundred feet away.

Emma glanced at the young clerk. No, he wouldn't understand.

"Never mind. I'll just call him." She held up her phone as if somehow Xavier's number might magically appear on her screen. Emma hustled away from the lobby counter, her face red with embarrassment. Even with a first name, she knew next to nothing about the man who'd made her come harder than anyone ever. Of course, now she knew his first name. Maybe she could find something on Google or Facebook? Maybe if she went home and tried, she might.

Emma rushed out to the dark Chicago night and hailed the first cab she saw, hoping that once she got home she might still be able to find the mystery man.

The next morning, after a few hours Googling "Xavier" and "tech" Emma came up with absolutely nothing. "Xavier" and "Chicago" yielded thousands of entries, none of whom seemed to fit Mr. X, though she discovered a local Xavier College, an apartment building and one restaurant. None of which were connected to Mr. X in any discernible way.

"This is so frustrating," Emma complained out loud as she set her coffee mug down on her desk with a little extra force. This was the digital age, after all, where all information was supposed to be a single Google search away. She'd never been in a position where a few clicks of the mouse wouldn't open up someone's whole identity.

Emma shook her head, scouring her memory for any little detail she could've missed about Mr. X, anything else she might type into Facebook, Instagram or Google. She couldn't think of any. The man had been deliberately vague about all the details of his life. She didn't know where he lived, worked, his last name, or even where he'd grown up. Then again, they hadn't spent a whole helluva lot of time talking, either, she remembered, a blush creeping up her cheeks.

I shouldn't even be doing this, Emma thought. *The man left me in the Ritz-Carlton bathroom, half naked! Clearly, all he wanted was sex.*

Not that she could blame him. The sex was freakin' amazing. The sex enough would be fine, yet, Emma couldn't shake the feeling there could be more than just physical attraction between them. She believed that amazing sex only happened with some kind of authentic emotional connection. They might be near strangers, but they had that connection. Somehow.

And he walked away from it.

She ought to be angry, but instead, she just felt mystified. Why had he bolted? Her mind went a thousand different directions: maybe she'd offended him somehow. Maybe he was really just using her and could *only* stand to be in her presence for the frantic minutes it took for sex?

But that didn't make any sense to her. He never let on he felt annoyed by her. *The first night, he'd held her all night long.*

No. It was almost as if he was fighting himself a little last night, but she couldn't say why.

Emma knew Xavier had been hurt, *knew* he wasn't looking for any commitment and he'd made it abundantly clear that he was only interested in knowing her for forty-eight hours. She ought to just face facts: he'd disappeared forever.

The thought suddenly depressed her. How could he walk away from something so…amazing? Surely, she wasn't the only one who felt like the sex was…well, white-hot. Surely he didn't have that kind of connection with every girl he met? Emma knew she'd never experienced sex like that her whole life.

She almost heard Sarah whispering, "You need to get laid more."

Emma sighed. Maybe it was that she'd only had a handful of boyfriends, all of them…well, on the boring side. She brushed away the thought. Why would Xavier be in such a hurry to leave?

Left on autopilot, her mind went to darker corners. Was he secretly married? His wife could have been *waiting outside in their car* while he came into the lobby of the hotel. Her palms grew clammy at the thought.

Emma typed in *Nost* and *married men* and about a dozen articles popped up on her screen. The headlines screamed at her: *Nost a Playground for Adulterers...* and *No Strings Doesn't Always Mean Single...*

Emma pored through the articles. Looks like *Nost* did have a cheater problem, with several spurned spouses—men and women—complaining about finding the app on the phone of their husband or wife. Could Xavier be one of them? It made sense: he was steadfastly attached to the "no contact" rule and guarded his last name with CIA-level dedication. Hell, his first name might not even be real.

She banged the edge of her desk in frustration. What was she supposed to do now?

Emma picked up her phone and noticed that her screen now included all new *Nost* men, none of whom were Mr. X. A search again found nothing, and there was no way to message him any longer.

She put her phone down. Emma stared at her computer for a beat and then pulled up a new Word document. Maybe if she couldn't find him, she could write about him. She began typing out her story about *Nost.* She worked on it furiously for the next couple of hours. She called it:

Mr. X, where are you?

When she'd poured out her emotions, doubts and fears onto the page, she sent off the draft to her editor and let out a breath. She had no idea if her article, written as PG as possible, was too risqué for the women's blog, but she was willing to take that chance. She crossed her fingers that somehow her little message in a bottle would make it to Xavier.

CHAPTER TEN

FOR THE REST of the week, Xavier felt…empty and alone. The feeling that he'd been making a huge mistake walking away from Emma at the Ritz-Carlton hadn't faded, and had only grown in its intensity. Rather than fade from his memory, Emma just loomed larger and larger, until almost every waking thought was of her. Her lips, her amazing curves, the softness of her skin. The way she simply *gave* herself to him, the completely vulnerable way she let him pleasure her. The out-of-this-world look on her face when she came for him.

Emma. What are you doing to me? He wondered, as he sat in his townhome in the west Loop, just blocks from his office. From his second-story bedroom window, he watched a couple walking together, hand-in-hand, down Jackson Boulevard, swinging their arms, happy as they laughed together beneath the unseasonably warm September sunshine on a bright Saturday afternoon. He envied their happiness, but he also felt it was all fake somehow. He knew that no matter how happy they seemed, beneath the surface trouble could be brewing. After all, Sasha held his hand, kissed him, even took him to bed while seeking the affection of another man.

Sure, all relationships started out filled with passion, but eventually they all petered out, under the weight of routine and familiarity. Or, they become something worse. Something harder. Like his parents' troubled relationship. He shook his head. No way was he going to become like his father, a slave to love.

He and Sasha had ripped their clothes off the night they met, but then a year later, beneath ratty old T-shirts and dozens of nights in the same bed, they had grown tired of one another, bored. Sex had become mechanical, predictable. No wonder she'd looked outside their relationship for satisfaction. He couldn't blame her. The passion that had once lit their relationship had fled.

Xavier pulled up his *Nost* profile on his phone but barely even looked at it. This was not like him at all. Normally, he was already on to his next challenge, his next anonymous rendezvous. The last year since Sasha had been a blur of bodies for the most part. He knew on some level it wasn't the healthiest way to get over his ex, but it sure was the most fun. Instead of browsing through the new candidates on his phone, he headed to the laptop in his study and once more pulled up Emma's profile. She'd been active in the last twenty-four hours, he saw, sending a little pang of jealousy through him. Had she already gotten over him? Was she trolling for new mates as he sat here at his computer?

His fingers froze on the keyboard. Would he snoop to find out? No. He shouldn't. That broke every privacy rule *Nost* had.

Get a hold of yourself, Xavier said. *What are you doing?*

He decided to Google her once more. That was safer than digging through her *Nost* profile—safer and not opening him or *Nost* up to a lawsuit, either, he mused. With a few quick clicks he discovered Emma had posted a new article for *Helena.* About *him.*

Interest piqued, he scanned the article.

Where is Mr. X? I never thought I'd ever use an app like Nost, or like it, but...

Xavier scanned the article, eating up every word. She enjoyed every minute of being with him, she said, enjoyed the freedom, the intimacy, the immediate connection. He knew they'd connected, but seeing it written in black and white delighted him. The way she described him was godlike. He grinned to himself. He hadn't even used *all* his best tricks. He still had some in reserve for…

When? When would he ever see her again? Their time was up. Forty-eight hours. That was his rule, but…

He glanced at her small profile picture that hovered above her article. Cornflower-blue eyes, lush blond hair, amazing pink lips. He remembered her small, pink nipples, the way they puckered beneath the caress of his tongue. Remembered below her waist, her delicate pink folds. He wanted to taste her again, make her arch her back and squirm with pleasure, see that amazing look in her eyes when she let the whole world go and embraced the climax he gave her.

He just wanted her.

He glanced once more at the end of the article.

Mr. X, if you're out there, find me at the Brew Coffee House. North Avenue. Four p.m. Saturday.

Xavier glanced at his watch. He had an hour to make it. If he really wanted to leave Emma in his past, stick to his rules, he'd let her wait. But he also felt desire growing inside him, a white-hot burn. She was asking for him. Could he really refuse?

By the time the fourth awkward, pimpled and overweight guy stumbled up to her and claimed to be *Mr. X* at the Brew Coffee House, Emma was beginning to think her idea to call out Mr. X publicly had backfired.

"You're not Mr. X," she told the twenty-something, acne-prone gamer who stood before her wearing a *Game of Thrones* T-shirt. He shuffled his massive feet.

"No, but I totally am!" he insisted, pushing up his flat-brimmed baseball cap to reveal unwashed, greasy hair beneath.

"You're not," she said, shaking her head. He didn't fight too much harder, and eventually shrugged and left. The cup of coffee she'd gotten half an hour ago now sat empty and she wondered how much longer she ought to keep this up. Mr. X clearly wasn't coming. He might not have even seen her article, and even if he did, might have chosen to ignore it. After all, he had the forty-eight-hour rule. No strings. No attachments.

But Emma wasn't asking to marry him. Just... explore him. A little longer. She just wasn't ready to let him go yet. He'd become a craving, more than that, an addiction. Something she didn't just *want,* she *needed.* The idea of going back to her boring, vanilla boyfriend sex life just felt horrible. She didn't want to do that. She wanted Mr. X.

Emma scribbled down a few notes on a notepad about *Game of Thrones* guy and figured that at least this would give her enough material for another article. Her *Helena* editor had *loved* the *Nost* piece, and no wonder, it was the top trending article on the blog and already had thousands of shares on social media. The article was blowing up, and Emma thought that was in no small part because more and more users were intrigued by *Nost*, and she was the good-girl-next-door who'd tried it and liked it. The story almost sold itself.

But then there was the thorny problem of Mr. X. Was he married? At least thirty percent of *Helena*'s readers thought so, if the comments on the post were any indication. *Keep moving, honey. He's married,* wrote one. Or, *Available men don't disappear like that. He probably has a wife and kids in the 'burbs,* wrote another. One woman had simply written *TOXIC BACHELOR* in the comments section and another wrote *escaped felon?* And he might be all these things. Or none of them.

Yet, deep inside, Emma just felt he wasn't. He was

a man who'd been hurt by love, betrayed by the one woman tasked with loving him above all others, and this was his way of dealing with it. She took what he said at face value. She knew she might not be able to change him, and probably couldn't. He'd flat-out told her he wasn't able to have a real relationship. Yet she couldn't shake the feeling that they belonged together. How many couples fit together so well? The sex wasn't just sex. At least not to her.

She might not be able to change him, she figured, but she just wanted to know him better. That's all.

She glanced around the near empty coffeehouse and sighed. This was a bust. An absolute bust. What a waste of time! Emma let out a long sigh as she gathered up her things, her flowered peasant top sliding down, revealing one bare shoulder. She wore a flouncy skirt and sandals, knowing that the warmth of this rare mild autumn afternoon would soon be traded for the chill of October. The summer seemed to be having one last hooray in September, but she knew the cold winds off Lake Michigan would arrive soon and they'd all settle in to coats and gloves for the rest of the season. She stood, about to leave, when a dark shadow fell over her table.

She glanced up to see Mr. X, wearing a simple dark T-shirt and cargo shorts. The T-shirt left nothing about his muscular chest to the imagination, and as she pulled her gaze away from his impressive muscles, she locked eyes with the man she'd been searching for for days.

"Xavier," she breathed, her heart thudding in her chest. "Where did you come from?"

"The door," he said smoothly and grinned. "Am I late?"

"Yes…er, n-no. Sit." Emma slumped back in her chair, feeling part shocked and part giddy. *He'd come. She'd called on him and he'd come.* "You…saw my story."

Xavier gave a single head nod, his golden hazel eyes never leaving hers as he slipped gracefully into the seat, all lean muscle, all stealth. "I especially enjoyed the part about…our kiss, but we did more than that."

"I—it had to be PG," she explained. How else to talk about how *Helena* wasn't the kind of magazine that published explicit sex.

"I liked our x-rated parts the best." Xavier flashed white teeth beneath his tanned face. The man was gorgeous, a dark-haired god. Emma forgot how much she felt the charismatic pull to him, and realized that she hadn't been crazy about letting this man do what he would with her—the electricity, the connection between them, couldn't be denied.

Xavier leaned forward. "Maybe we ought to retreat to the bathroom?" He let the offer hang there, and Emma's mind went straight back to the Ritz-Carlton, where he'd taken her, panting, inside the stall. She'd never done anything like that her whole life, yet as soon as he mentioned it, her whole body tingled in anticipation. Then she remembered—The Brew didn't have bathrooms.

"No bathrooms here," she said, of the tiny little coffeehouse with only a couple of tables. The counter took up one whole wall of the establishment, and then windows and the door were on the opposite. The bathroom, if there was one, was for employees only.

"That's a shame." Xavier's hand snaked out under the table and rested on her knee, and she could feel the heat and the heaviness of his hand through the thin fabric. He then moved his hand beneath her skirt, his hand touching the bare skin of her inner thigh. She sucked in a breath. Here, in the middle of a public shop, he had his hand up her skirt. He stroked her inner thigh, inching ever higher. Emma's heart beat harder as Xavier's index finger reached the fabric of her panties. He gently laid pressure through the thin fabric, a temptation, a promise.

Emma had never wished for a bathroom so much in her life. She could feel her insides turning to warm mush, her arousal growing as his finger gently probed her through the fabric, which, she thought, had to be drenched. A patron came in through the front door then and Xavier withdrew his hand, and Emma felt its cold absence. Now her body was abuzz with a million wants, and the man who could fulfill them leaned back in his chair across the table and took a sip of coffee, calm as ever.

"Are you married?" Emma blurted, suddenly.

Xavier nearly spit out his coffee. "No."

"In a relationship? Pregnant girlfriend at home?"

"No! Of course not. I'm on *Nost*." He acted as if the idea was preposterous.

"I read about married men…and women…seeking… fun on *Nost.* It's a perfect cover, right? No names, no strings, no way of your spouse finding out you're cheating." Emma's voice was rising and she worked hard to keep it down. *Keep calm.*

"Well, that's unfortunate that some are not who they say they are." Xavier frowned. "I'm sure that's not what *Nost* intended. In fact, I think it says something about that in the user agreement."

Emma waved her hands, not caring about the fine print of *Nost.* "Why did you run out on me?" This was the hardest question, and she wasn't even sure she wanted to know the answer. "At the Ritz-Carlton?"

Xavier studied her a moment. "I was scared," he finally admitted, shifting uncomfortably in his chair and not meeting her gaze.

"Scared?" Emma didn't understand.

"I…want more from you. More than forty-eight hours."

Emma's heart leaped. "That's exactly what I want." She leaned forward and grabbed both his hands with hers. "Why don't we do that? Here… Here's my phone number." She frantically scribbled on the pad of paper, gave him her name and phone number. "You can give me yours, and we can start there." He stared at the paper on the table. But instead of looking excited, he looked…sad.

"Emma, if we continue on, this relationship won't last," he said.

She felt as if he'd struck her, the pain, the disappointment sliced through her. Did he not like her as much as she liked him after all? "What do you mean?"

He squeezed her hand and studied her hand linked in his. "It'll grow old. All relationships do. It'll get comfortable. Predictable. Or worse, volatile." He spoke as if the words left a bitter taste in his mouth. "And then, regardless, boring or volatile, you or I…will stray. That's what happens."

"Not to *all* relationships," Emma protested.

"To all the ones I've had," he said, and she saw the fresh pain of his fiancée's betrayal on his face.

"But you can't assume all women are like…her." She wasn't Sasha. How could she prove it? "I'm not the kind of woman to cheat."

Xavier laughed, a bitter, hollow sound. "Emma, all people can cheat, given the right circumstances. People aren't like penguins. We don't mate for life. People get bored, they get tired, they get frustrated. I'm not so sure it's possible to have a healthy, monogamous relationship."

Emma sighed in frustration. None of what he told her was exactly new. Hadn't he admitted after they first met that that's why he liked *Nost* so much? Why was she surprised to find a commitment-phobic man on *Nost*? Yet she just couldn't give up on the connection they had. She wasn't ready to walk away yet.

"But don't you want to explore…this?" She gestured

between the two of them with her free hand. “You can’t have this—what I’m feeling—with just anyone.”

That made Xavier pause and think. Right then she knew he felt more than he was saying. He felt their strong bond, too. This was more than just white-hot sex, more than just two people wildly attracted to one another. Something real lay beneath, something that felt like they’d met before. Emma didn’t believe in reincarnation, but if she did, she’d swear they’d met in a previous life.

“This…is real,” Emma said, squeezing his hand tighter.

“If you knew me, if you *really* knew me, then all of this…this chemistry…would disappear.” Xavier sounded so sure.

“How can you be so sure? I mean, it might. You’re right. There’s a risk it could. But what if it didn’t?” Emma shifted her legs beneath the table and her knee touched his. She could feel the electric current of want flow between them and as he leaned in, she knew he felt it, too.

“Want to go for a walk?” he asked her.

CHAPTER ELEVEN

EMMA WALKED BESIDE Xavier down the crowded street of North Avenue, strangers passing them, seemingly unaware of the current running between the couple. The late-afternoon air had turned cooler, as the sun dipped below the horizon, setting a blue tint to everything. Night was coming, but it wasn't quite here yet. The slight breeze ruffled the changing leaves as a few yellow ones fell at their feet. Emma could almost feel it: a force field of desire, a pull between them. He was the earth and she was the moon, attached by gravity, an invisible force, aware of every little move he made.

As they walked, he slipped his hand over hers, possessive, a promise.

"I already knew about you, Emma Allaire," Xavier said suddenly.

"What do you mean?" she asked, thinking about the paper she'd scribbled in the coffee shop. The paper that Xavier hadn't taken. She'd folded it and tucked it in her bag.

"I searched you on Google," he admitted. "You told

me the magazine where you worked, so it wasn't hard to find you. Your Facebook page is set to public, by the way. Did you intend that?"

Emma felt hot suddenly. He'd searched for her? Just as she'd searched for him. Then, of course, he had to: after all, he'd found her at the coffee shop, hadn't he? Read the article she wrote? But the fact that he was admitting to wanting to know more about her, admitting to not being satisfied with them being perfect strangers, linked only in carnal knowledge, went against his life philosophy, didn't it? Maybe she was getting to him, tearing down the walls he'd built to protect himself, to keep her out.

"You broke your own rules, then." Emma felt strangely smug in pointing that out.

Xavier gave her a sidelong glance, his eyes looking almost golden in the autumn sunlight. "Yes," he admitted. "You intrigued me."

"You intrigued me, too. I searched you as well. But you gave me nothing to go on."

Xavier chuckled, low in his throat. "I know."

"Give me one detail. Just one."

The two passed a narrow alleyway between two brownstones. Xavier pulled her into it and around the corner, protected by a Dumpster on one side and a brick wall partition on the other. "Kiss me first," he demanded, voice low, a gravelly whisper.

Her lips parted, and all she could do was nod her head. Xavier swooped down, claiming her mouth, and suddenly the heat flared between them, their mouths and tongues wrapped together in an ancient mating dance of want and desire. God, she wanted him, the passion flaring, her need growing as he delved into her mouth again and again. They devoured each other, the passion like none she'd ever experienced. Was it because she knew that he could disappear from her life at any moment? Was it because he *was* a stranger? A man who stubbornly refused to open himself up to her? To give her a detail as small as his last name? Could it be that he was a blank canvas, someone she could project everything on to, the perfect man?

She didn't know. All she knew in that moment was that her body became a melted puddle of want, that in that moment, passion made her a slave. She'd do whatever he asked, whenever he asked it in that second. She'd long forgotten about the people passing by just around the corner on the sidewalk, or the fact that in the alley, even in the darkening dusk, they could still be seen by a row of condo windows. She didn't care who saw them. All she wanted was more of his mouth and his hands, as they roamed her body. She might not know his name, but she knew his hands, the sure way they possessed her, stroked her, made her beg for more. Emma suddenly didn't care that she was in public, in the darkening dusk, partially hidden and yet still visible. All she cared about was getting more of Xavier, of not wanting this moment to end.

"I want you. Here," Xavier growled in her ear, and

then his hands were inside the thin lace of her thong, feeling how much she wanted him, too. "I want you now."

All thoughts of caution fled her mind. She was just a pulsating nerve of want, nothing more. She'd never done anything like this before: in public, barely covered by the darkening light. Yet, she wanted him just as much as he wanted her. She pushed her own thong off her hips and it dropped to the ground. She felt the coolness of the night air slide between her thighs. She felt exposed, but it only added to her desire, her want. She was ready. Suddenly, Xavier lifted her, pressing her against the brick wall of the alley, taking her with his whole self. She gasped with shock and pleasure, instinctively wrapping her legs around his waist as he pushed inside her, his eyes meeting hers, the want in them as strong as her own. Emma took him all, feeling reckless, feeling how deliciously wrong this was: a stranger, an alley, herself, exposed to anyone who happened by, doing the thing good girls never did. Good girls never did this with strangers, in public. Yet, here she was, spreading her legs eagerly, letting him in, ready for him; the combination of adrenaline and want sent her instantly over the edge, as she hit a ragged climax, swallowing the shout of pleasure in her throat.

Xavier came as well, in a last urgent and shuddering thrust before quickly withdrawing.

"I want a detail," she murmured to him in the dark, grabbing a fistful of his shirt. "I want to know your last name."

"If you knew that, you wouldn't have come for me so hard," he warned, voice low as he zipped up. "You wouldn't have let me take you here."

"You promised a detail," she pressed. "For a kiss. And I gave you more than a kiss." She was still panting as Xavier glanced back and forth, looking for witnesses. Then he leaned forward and whispered the digits of a phone number in her ear. He kissed her hard and left her wanting more.

Emma memorized the digits, repeating them in her head long after they'd gone separate ways from the alley. She watched as Xavier moved down the crowded public sidewalk. She was spent and sore, feeling like she might be standing on the edge of a precipice with no way down. Should she follow him? She felt weak-kneed and spent. Had she just fucked him in public? In full view of the condo window across the alley? She'd no idea if someone had seen, and she hurried on her way down the block and back to the safety of her own condo, so quickly she'd abandoned her thong on the concrete ground. She wondered what on earth had come over her. But then she knew what had: Xavier. His hands, his steady hazel eyes, his jet-black hair. The way he fit inside her perfectly, seemed to hit every nerve ending in her body all at once.

Was he right? Was the chemistry between them just because they were strangers? Emma didn't feel this with the men she saw on the sidewalk, or on the train, or passing her in the aisle of the grocery store. Being strangers didn't automatically mean chemistry. She stuck resolutely to her belief that she and Xavier shared something: a past life, a spiritual connection, *something* that made the sex so amazingly mind-blowing, that made her want him so badly that she took off her thong in an alley for him, let him inside her in the darkening dusk.

Would the sex be as wild, be as amazing, if they were a couple? Sleeping over in each other's beds, knowing the ins and outs of each other's routines? She thought about her past boyfriends, about knowing all the little details: the sound of their snores, their favorite Thai takeout dishes, their childhood stories. Had that made the sex…boring as well? Predictable?

The more sex she had with Xavier, the more… unpredictable, hotter, it got. She'd never in a million years guess she'd let him take her against a brick wall outside, just a few feet from a bustling city street, yet she had. She'd wanted it as much as he had. Was that because she didn't know him? Would knowing him make her too shy, too embarrassed to do those things?

Emma wondered. Still, it didn't stop her from immediately typing in the phone number he'd given her to try to find its owner. Every site she tried came up with a dead end. The number, whatever it was, wasn't registered to anyone. A burner phone? Maybe.

She decided to text it and find out.

I want to know your last name, she texted.

Well, hello to you, kitten, Xavier wrote back almost instantly, as if he'd been waiting for her. I enjoyed you today. Did you enjoy me?

Yes, she typed, her fingers trembling slightly as she remembered the passion with which he took her just a half hour ago.

I love the way you feel. You were made for me.

And you for me, she typed. I've never done that before. Outside. In public.

I know, he wrote, as if he could read her mind. But, that's what can happen between two strangers. No inhibitions.

You're not a stranger to me, she said. I know what you like. How you come. Your body. She knew how he came, the look on his face of pure release. She knew the little shuddering movement he made when he was done, a little hiccup unique to him, and the rush of air from his lungs when he did. That made them less than strangers. She knew he never came before she did, she knew he was always determined to please her first. She knew his touch drove her wild.

You already know too much.

I want to know more, she furiously typed back.

And then, Mr. X went quiet. No more texts. Emma stared at her phone, wondering where he'd gone. To work? She had no idea where he even worked. There were dozens of tech companies, and he'd been deliberately vague. Home to his wife?

He'd said he wasn't married. She believed him, and yet…he seemed so extremely commitment-phobic for a man who'd only lost a fiancée. Sure, that was traumatic, but this felt so…extreme. Emma wondered about that. Was there an extreme form of commitment phobia? Was it a *condition*? She ran a quick Google search.

"Relationship anxiety," she read aloud, skimming a few psychology articles. "…in its most extreme forms means a person is afraid to make a real commitment to another. This can be caused by the end of a relationship they didn't see coming, or, in some cases, childhood trauma."

Emma paused then. Childhood trauma? Could this be it?

She skimmed further. Most often, she read, sufferers of extreme commitment phobia failed to have secure bonding with one or both parents, or they might have been hurt by someone they trusted, a relative or caregiver. "Sometimes," she read, "those with the severest cases of relationship anxiety often show conflicting signs: they might be passionate one minute, and aloof the next."

Emma nodded her head with conviction. That was Xavier in a nutshell.

"To cure relationship anxiety, the sufferer often needs to confront his or her past and understand that those traumas might not be repeated in the present," she read aloud. She wondered if it would be that easy? She shut off her computer. Was she really going to diagnose his psychological failings by Google? Wasn't she projecting her own thoughts and worries *onto* him? That's what happened when she didn't know him. All she could do was guess.

I want to see you. Dinner tonight? She tried.

Emma stared at her screen but saw nothing. No reply. Had she lost him? Was he just in an aloof phase? Still, she couldn't shake the feeling that her fishing line had gone slack and he'd cut bait.

Xavier stared at his burner phone, the one he only used for *Nost,* at Emma's invitation. Every fiber of his body wanted to say yes, wanted to see her again, smell her lavender shampoo once more, feel her again: soft, wet and willing. But the very need that rose in his chest scared him. He hadn't felt this needy since growing up as a child, alone in his room, his father desperately trying to talk his mother down from one of her rages. Later, of course, he'd know it was that she was bipolar, but that would only come after. He buried those memories of his mother so very deeply that he wondered why he thought of her now. She'd died when he was just nine. His memories of her seemed vague at best, though he knew that sometimes she was vibrant, energized, unstoppable, the brightest star in the room, not caring who she burnt, and other times, she wouldn't leave her bed for days at a time. Papi remained loyal to her her whole life, and when he questioned why, his father told him, *you can't choose who you love.* The old romantic. Look what it had gotten him: a troubled marriage, the early death of his wife, almost a whole lifetime living without her.

He shook the thought away. He could choose *not* to love, couldn't he? He shut off his burner phone and tucked it into his pocket, vowing not to look at it for the rest of the week.

CHAPTER TWELVE

EMMA TOOK A deep swig of her gin and tonic as she sat at the crowded bar in the heart of Wrigleyville. Outside, the sidewalks were thick with bar hoppers, and the air was chilled with coming fall. The Cubs had long since finished their game at nearby Wrigley Field, though the revelers hung on, still celebrating the first post-season victory.

"You need to let him go," Sarah advised, as she took a sip of her vodka soda. She wore her red hair up in a messy bun, and a slinky sweater, skinny jeans and open-toed ankle boots that showed off a new cherry-red pedicure. "He's been AWOL for a week, he probably gave you a burner number and, anyway, he's not responding… I mean, the writing is on the wall."

"But…we *had* something," Emma protested, staring moodily into her glass. She'd barely paid attention to her outfit: a slouchy sweater that kept sliding off one shoulder and black leggings. She wore her hair loose and naturally dried, the natural waves showing through. The vibe around them was boisterous and loud, but Emma just felt isolated and alone. Despite being surrounded by attractive men, she only wanted to think about Xavier.

"You mean you *had* amazing sex," Sarah corrected, thumping her glass down on the bar for emphasis. "And you never know, it could've gone south when you found out he still lives in his mom's basement and spends his off time smoking weed."

"He doesn't do that!"

"How do you know?" Sarah arched an eyebrow and Emma sighed. She didn't know, not really. She didn't know the man's last name, much less where he lived.

"It's driving me insane. You can find *anything* out about *anybody* these days just on your phone!" Emma waved her smartphone in the air. "But he's a black box. It's just not right."

"Maybe it's better this way," Sarah cautioned as she took another small sip of her drink. "Maybe he's bad news. Gang-banger?"

"No!" Emma exclaimed.

"Okay, white-collar felon." Sarah took a little sip of her vodka soda, shaking it so the ice cubes clinked against the side of the glass.

Emma shook her head. "He's just…troubled."

"Mental issues?"

"Commitment issues. Relationship anxiety."

Sarah shoved her shoulder. "Have you been Google diagnosing again?"

Emma gave a guilty shrug.

"You know that stuff is dangerous!" Sarah cried, putting her glass down on the bar. "By the time you were on the outs with Devin, you were convinced he had a borderline personality." Sarah rolled her eyes.

"He does!" Emma exclaimed.

Sarah heaved a frustrated sigh. "You need to close WebMD, and start facing facts. Mr. X is gone, but that's okay. He wasn't the staying type."

Emma remembered how quickly he'd left her the last two times they'd been together. He'd been in such a rush to leave her he'd barely said goodbye. Staying was absolutely not his strong suit.

"And he's gone radio silent for a week. It's done, sweetie. I know you want there to be something there, but there's just not." Sarah gave Emma's shoulders a reassuring squeeze. "Doesn't mean you can't find someone else."

Emma stared morosely at her drink. She didn't want someone else. She wanted Xavier. "What if he got into a car accident…? What if he really does want to contact me, but…"

Sarah let out a long, frustrated sigh. "Honey, that isn't what happened. This is *Nost*. No strings, remember? That's what you signed on for!"

"I know, but…"

"You just need to shift gears a little. Quit focusing on one man. What you need is a distraction. Give me your phone," Sarah demanded, holding her palm up.

"Why?"

"Just…gimme." Sarah opened and closed her hand

impatiently. Reluctantly, Emma set her phone in her friend's hand. In seconds, Sarah had pulled up *Nost* and all active members within a half-mile radius.

"No, no, no!" Emma cried, reaching out and trying to grab her phone back, but Sarah held it just out of reach.

"This is for your own good," Sarah said, sending out a few winks to nearby suitors. She glanced up around the bar, looking hopeful.

"I don't want to meet anyone else!"

"You might not *want* to, but you *need* to." Sarah typed a message to one member Emma couldn't even see.

"Who are you messaging? What..."

"Just trust me," Sarah exclaimed as she grinned into the phone.

"Let me *see.*" Emma reached out and tugged on Sarah's arm.

"I'm just saying hi to a few nearby possibilities." She peered at the screen. "Oh, my, there are like *dozens!*"

Given that they were in a sports bar surrounded by guys, that didn't surprise Emma in the least. "Show me."

Eventually, Sarah pulled up a few profiles. "See? He's not so bad."

Emma looked at the blond guy who was slim but not fit, kind of cute but no Xavier. She saw his hazel eyes in her mind, his jet-black hair, the look on his face when he pulled her in for a kiss... Then, she felt herself dissolve a little. How could he walk away from that? From *them*?

Sarah showed her another. "Hey, you got a new message from Good Lookin' Good Times. He looks kind of familiar. Did we message him?"

"What?" Emma glanced down at the screen, her Xavier revelry broken. That's when she saw the fake profile picture that Happy Fun Time had used, the man who'd been so nasty to her at the Ritz-Carlton bar.

"That's Happy Fun Time!" Emma exclaimed, swiping the photo so it got bigger. "I mean, that's not *him,* him, but it's the fake photo he used. Trust me, he looks nothing like that *GQ* model." She studied the map on the phone. "It says he's *right* near us, too."

Emma glanced around hurriedly. Then, seconds later, she saw a telltale Cardinals cap in the back corner of the bar, by the pool tables.

"Oh, God! There he is! Cardinals hat?" Emma told Sarah, trying to covertly side nod with her head.

"The old guy? Seriously overweight?" Sarah wrinkled her nose. "That is false advertising."

"I know." Emma stirred her drink. "Don't stare," she admonished, suddenly fearful the man would see them. He must know they were nearby. He'd messaged her, but maybe there was a chance he hadn't seen them yet. The bar was crowded, and Emma cringed, using the men behind her as a shield.

"And who in their right mind wears a St. Louis hat to a Cubs game?"

"He's a jerk, so who knows?" Emma shrugged, remembering the vile way he'd clutched at her elbow, the coldness of his voice when he'd hissed *bitch* in her face.

"He's the guy that grabbed you, right?" Sarah's frown deepened. "Let's report him," she suggested, quickly clicking on the "report user" button, and she tapped in their complaint. She made sure to write *false advertising* in all caps, as well as *belligerent* and *rude* and *assault.*

"Maybe we should go," Emma suggested, suddenly feeling uncomfortable. She didn't want the man to find them.

"Fine. I got this round." Sarah slapped down a few bills in the small shot glass that held their bill, and then they made their way through the thick crowd to the exit.

They were barely out the door when behind them, someone shouted, "Hey, Kitten!"

Emma froze, for a second, wondering if it was Mr. X.

But, when she turned, she found the average-looking blond with two of his friends. "Kitten, you're even prettier in person. We were going in to Barleycorn." He nodded at the big Irish pub near them. "Buy you and your friend a drink?"

Sarah gave Emma nudge.

"Okay," Emma reluctantly agreed.

Xavier sat at his laptop at home, poring over a bug in the *Nost* code that some of his engineers couldn't figure out. He'd spent the week burying himself in work, trying to stave off thoughts of Emma: what she was doing, what she was wearing, who she might be with. He'd resolutely refused to answer her query about dinner, and yet, he worried that she might be giving up on *him.* After all, he'd never responded, but she hadn't followed up, either. Her question sat on his phone, almost like a dare, a challenge. So far, he'd resisted caving, but he could feel his fingers itching to respond. Itching to set a time and place.

Only work could keep him from doing that. He had to throw himself into work and hope that eventually he'd forget about Emma.

You don't forget about the woman you love, his father had told him. He hated that his father's voice seemed to be in his head constantly. *I don't love her, Papi,* he wanted to say, *I don't even know her.*

Yet, why did he suddenly understand why his father kept coming back to his erratic mother? Why else would he suffer so much?

Emma doesn't seem like suffering, though, an inner voice of reason said. *Emma is passionate, vulnerable, whole. She's not Mama. Or Sasha.*

Sasha. The moment she betrayed him, Xavier saw his mother all over again: the woman who burned so brightly, she burned everyone around her, too. He might have been young, just eight, but he remembered the nights his father would go out looking for his mother, the worried look on Xavier's aunt's face as she tried to reassure him that everything was fine. He knew everything wasn't fine.

Xavier blinked away the memory of the frightened little boy. He was a man now, a man in charge of his own destiny. And he wasn't going to be weak like his father.

In fact, he'd prove it. He pulled up the *Nost* app on his phone. Beautiful women smiled back at him from his inbox. Yet, even as he pored through the pictures, all he could do was compare each and every one of them to Emma. They all came up wanting. Why couldn't he get her out of his mind? Why couldn't he put aside thoughts of her? He would find a way to rid himself of this desire, of this *weakness*. He wouldn't be his father. He forced himself to message a gorgeous brunette and a beautiful twenty-something. He needed a palate cleanser, that's all, he reasoned. The second he had another woman, he'd forget all about Emma. Wouldn't he? He put his phone down and turned his attention back to his screen.

As he typed on his computer, he saw a notice coming into his inbox. He'd signed on to be copied on all complaints registered at *Nost.* He opened the message, and that's when he saw Emma's account flick before his eyes. She was active again? was his first thought. A flame of jealousy rose up in his chest. Was she, right now, in the arms of another man?

The thought of her flirting…or kissing…another man, made him shift uncomfortably in his office chair. He didn't like that idea. Not one bit.

Then he read her complaint, and as soon as he pulled up the profile picture of the guy, he knew it was the same man who'd hassled her at the bar. He'd put up the exact same fake photo of himself, and the description she'd typed of him—down to the St. Louis Cardinals baseball cap—all rang a bell. *Dammit,* the asshole had slipped into the system again.

This time, Xavier dug deeper. He pulled up the man's fake profile, but, unlike other profiles, he'd actually put in a local phone number. After being booted from the system multiple times, he'd be locked out, unless he used a number that worked, a number he could confirm by text. This could be Xavier's break. He used reverse look-up online for the number, and found it registered to a Jimmy Keith. Could it be that easy? Was Jimmy Keith the man? Or would it be another dead end?

Xavier ran a few more searches on him, and landed on a social media page, which confirmed it: this was the guy who'd bullied Emma at the bar. He had only a handful of Facebook friends, but was born and raised in St. Louis. Xavier went a step further and ran the man's name through a criminal background check. Results instantly popped up: trespassing, public intoxication—and then Xavier saw something that made the room spin. He had pleaded guilty to sexual assault ten years ago in St. Louis. Another Google search pulled up local newspaper articles about it. He was sentenced to eight years, but was paroled early.

This piece of shit had managed to get into *Nost* at least twice and was right now in it again, preying on unsuspecting women.

This asshole had grabbed Emma's arm at the bar.

Xavier felt his blood boil as he called his friend, the

Chicago detective. He didn't know if there was anything that could be done, but he sure as hell would find out. He got voice mail and left a message. He pulled up some of Emma's messages and realized the ex-con had tried to message Emma again, this time under his new profile. Xavier wished he could pull up her location, but even he couldn't do that from the code in his office. He'd need a new profile on *Nost*, and fast, in order to find her and even then, that might take too long.

But he had to warn her, he thought. If Emma was anywhere near this man, he had to find her. The man was dangerous.

CHAPTER THIRTEEN

EMMA SAT WITH the friendly, but a little bit bland, guys who'd bought drinks for them. She was pretty sure two of them were interested in Sarah, but one—the blond with the average build—was absolutely fixated on her. He kept finding reasons to touch her, which Emma wasn't so sure she liked. He seemed nice enough. Casey, who lived around the corner in an apartment he shared with the two friends he was with, was working a low-level accounting job, but hoping for advancement. They were exactly the same age, but somehow that just didn't feel quite right. His friends kept trying to order Jäger shots, which just made Emma's stomach turn. Clearly, these fellas hadn't left the college binge-drinking scene behind just yet. The way they slammed beers made Emma think about frat parties and keg stands. She sighed. She missed Mr. X: his sophistication, the way he seemed...beyond all the immaturity.

Except for the fact that Mr. X wouldn't even give you his real name, a voice in her head reminded her. At least Casey here gave his full name right off the bat.

And she knew so much about him already in the first five minutes: Boston College grad, licensed accountant, loved college football and camping. Wanted to take her sometime, he said, to Starved Rock, his favorite local campground. Emma tried to muster up some interest, but just failed. He was nice enough, but just dull.

Then, she wondered if it was because she knew too much about him. Had Mr. X been right? Did knowledge make a person…boring?

"One time when we were camping…" Casey continued, happy to steer the conversation, as Emma nodded and smiled weakly. As Casey spoke, relating some tale about raccoons getting into his cooler and stealing a beer, Emma tried to block out his voice. She studied his blue eyes, his average, but somewhat cute face, and wondered: Would she have sex with this man in an alley at dusk? In a public restroom at a fancy hotel?

Inwardly, she shook her head. It didn't matter if she knew everything about him or nothing, she decided. Casey just didn't light that spark in her.

Mr. X was different. Special, somehow. He had to know that.

"And then we found that he'd somehow *popped the top of the can.* Can you believe that? Raccoons, man… they are smarter than you think."

Casey finished his story and Emma laughed politely. She glanced at Sarah and couldn't tell whether or not she enjoyed the attention of Casey's friends. Would she be up for bailing? Now? Sarah flipped her red hair off one shoulder. Looked like she might be flirting with one of them…or hell, both, for all Emma knew.

"Well, this guy needs to go drain the snake," Casey said, getting up from his bar stool. Emma flinched a little at the vernacular. Did he have to say it *that* way?

Emma just nodded and Casey sauntered into the crowd, looking for the men's room. Emma felt her phone buzz in her pocket and she tugged it out of her jacket. She glanced at the face and saw a text from Mr. X.

Where are you?

She felt a ripple of anticipation run through her. He hadn't contacted her for a week! Emma thought Sarah had been right—he'd been done and it was time to face facts: that whatever they had was just a temporary thing. But, here, on her phone, was proof that Mr. X hadn't walked away. Not just yet, anyway. And he hadn't been in a car accident, either. No, here he was on her phone.

Emma felt such relief, such joy, that he'd contacted her, she immediately started typing a reply. I'm drinking at…

Then she paused. He'd kept her at bay for a whole week. Kept her wondering, kept her hanging. She had every reason to be angry at him, she reasoned. She thought she might never see him again! He *let* her think that. Besides, if she let him in, if she invited him out, they'd just end up with steamy, amazing sex, and then he'd probably just disappear again. Is that what she wanted? No, she decided. Not this time.

Why do you want to know? she responded, instead.

I need to see you, he typed, almost instantly.

Her heart sang a bit. He needed to see her! *Probably just for a quick hookup,* that little voice in her head said. And then, another quickly replied, *And what's wrong with that?* She felt her thighs tingle. He knew how to satisfy her, that was for sure. The sex would be amazing, even if it was of the wham, bam, thank-you, ma'am variety. She wanted that, but she also wanted to know his full name. And he owed her that much. This time, she wouldn't let him arrive, seduce her with his amazing charisma and expert hands. No, this time, she'd get what she needed *before* she saw him.

On one condition, she typed.

Emma, please. Just tell me where you are! That guy—the one who harassed you at the bar the night we met—I know he's trying to message you. He's dangerous, so do not meet him anywhere!

Emma read Xavier's message and frowned. How did he know the man was messaging her? Did he know the Cardinals hat guy? Emma already knew he was dangerous from her run-in with him at the Ritz-Carlton, but what did Xavier mean?

I just saw him but I don't think he saw me, Emma texted back. How did you know he messaged me?

Turn off your Nost location finder, he told her once more. He could find you.

Emma felt a chill run down her spine. Quickly, she hit "location-off" on her app.

Where are you? Xavier asked once more, ignoring her inquiry.

First you have to tell me your first AND last name. Now let him try to worm his way out of this one. At least she'd make him work for it.

She stared at her phone and saw he was typing. His answer popped up on her screen:

Xavier Pena. Where are you?

She felt a surge of satisfaction. There. She knew his name now, and he wouldn't be able to disappear so quickly from her life. Not now.

Casey had returned from the bar but she only barely looked up from her phone as she tapped out her response: John Barleycorn.

Stay there, he responded. I'm on my way.

Emma felt a surge of excitement. He was coming out! She was going to see him—the elusive Mr. X. Now she knew his name, as well. *Xavier Pena.* She itched to Google him, but Casey was in front of her once more.

"So, tell me about *you,*" Casey said. "I've been talking this whole time. What's a gorgeous girl like you doing on *Nost*? You could have any guy at this bar with a snap of your fingers."

She squirmed at the compliment and felt a bit of guilt. After all, she was not going home with Casey tonight, not if Mr. X, Xavier, was on his way. *Xavier*

Pena. The name suited him. And she'd be Googling him at the first available opportunity. She glanced at the door of the bar and saw the revolving doors swing around. Was Xavier here already?

But then, she saw the telltale red baseball brim. *Cardinals hat.* He was back. Had he found her before she turned off her location finder on *Nost*?

Emma crouched down, trying to use Casey as a shield. "Everything okay?" he asked her.

"Uh, just someone I don't want to see," Emma said. Casey turned to look at the front of the bar. Emma took the opportunity to reach out and grab Sarah's elbow and tug her close. "Cardinals Hat is here," Emma whispered in her friend's ear. Sarah craned her neck and saw the man working his way through the crowd. Suddenly, the man lifted his head and through the crowd, managed to make eye contact with Emma. She wanted to look away, but she found herself frozen, unable to move. The man's lip curled up in a cruel smile of recognition. Emma knew in that minute that he had been looking for her, and that his intentions were anything but good. She felt a cold chill run down her spine, all of her instincts telling her to get away from that man.

"Who is that guy?" Casey asked.

"An asshole," Sarah responded. "Don't worry. We'll make sure he doesn't come near you."

Emma was thankful for the offer, and yet, despite her presence and the dozens of other people in the bar, she still felt vulnerable, exposed.

"Want another round?" Casey asked her suddenly, but all Emma wanted to do was to get out of the bar, away from the man who now took up a position leaning against a column in her direct line of sight. He wasn't coming up to her, and she guessed she ought to be grateful for that, but the way he just stood across the bar, staring at her, made her even more uncomfortable. She just wanted to get out of his line of sight. She couldn't shake the feeling that in his mind, he was plotting terrible things to do to her. She knew that sounded crazy, but she felt that he might become violent and that if he caught her alone she might be in serious danger.

Then Xavier came through the doors. She saw him first, and then their eyes met. Emma felt relief and more seeing his handsome self, clad in a simple black T-shirt, windbreaker and jeans, looking dark and dangerous as his tall and imposing figure cut through the crowd. Emma nodded to her left, toward her stalker, and Xavier saw him at the same time.

"Jimmy!" he shouted, which got the man's attention. He turned, saw Xavier, and then suddenly bolted for the back, shoving bar-goers out of his way. He pushed one woman to the ground who fell hard, spilling her drink on a group of guys standing next to her.

"Hey!" one of them cried, and then Cardinals Hat had more than one pursuer, as the girl's boyfriend gave chase.

Stymied by the thick crowd, Xavier couldn't catch Jimmy. Emma watched as the man disappeared through the back. Xavier followed and Emma, worried about him, bolted for the back as well.

"Where are you..." she heard the blond shout after her, but she was already gone, worried about Xavier. She wiggled through the crowd, and before she knew it, found herself at the back kitchen, where Xavier had stopped by an open alleyway door.

"He's gone," he told her, running his hands through his thick hair. "I went out there, and...I don't know, he's just gone."

Emma felt a bit of relief. Xavier was safe, the jerk was gone.

Xavier turned, looking at her with a pained expression. "Emma, that man...he's got a sexual assault conviction on his record."

"He...what?" Emma tried to process that information. "But he was certified with a background check." The noise from the clang of pots and pans in the kitchen and the low rumble of music from the bar made it so Emma had to raise her voice.

Xavier shook his head. "He got past the safeguards somehow, but I'm going to figure out how and stop him. Put in more security. Something. I'm working on it, but, Emma, I'm sorry."

She wasn't sure she'd heard right over the noise in the bar.

"Why are you sorry? And what do you mean, 'working on it'?" Now Emma was beyond confused. What was he talking about?

Xavier hung his head. He glanced around as if he wasn't sure how to break bad news. Then he caught her eye once more, his own eyes fixed on hers, deliberate and serious.

"You'll find out with your first Google search, anyway." He sighed, shaking his head. "I built *Nost*. I own it."

CHAPTER FOURTEEN

Emma felt like the earth suddenly tilted beneath her feet and she had trouble steadying herself.

"You *own Nost*?" A million confused questions raced through her mind, none of them good. Had he gamed the system? Had this somehow been just an elaborate joke?

Xavier nodded his head once.

"You use your *own* app to pick up girls?"

A flash of guilt crossed his face. "What kind of hypocrite would I be if I made the app but didn't use it?" Xavier was trying to be lighthearted, to joke, but Emma found nothing about this to be funny.

Somehow, it just seemed all wrong that he was using his own app, his own program, to find women, but Emma couldn't say why. Maybe it was because he'd be able to game the system (he created it, so he'd have to know how to take advantage, right?) or maybe it was because his commitment phobia went far, far deeper than she ever realized.

"You *created Nost*." She just couldn't get over the

fact that the man she was falling for had relationship anxiety so deep that he built a company around it. There might never be a cure for him. All of her hopes about them *being something more* felt like they disintegrated in that moment. *Poof,* up in fantasy fairy-tale smoke.

"Yes." Xavier moved closer and she backed away until she was flat against the wall in the corridor between the kitchen and the bathroom. "I told you up front that no strings was what I wanted."

Yes, he had. He'd been more than up front about that. So why did it bother her so much that he owned *Nost*?

It was because he was here and he knew the man in the Cardinals hat would be here. He also knew the man was messaging her. But how?

"How did you know that man would be here tonight?" She pointed toward the back door where the jerk had fled.

Now Xavier looked uncomfortable. He rubbed the back of his neck. "I looked at your account," he admitted.

"You can see the messages?" Now Emma felt shocked. He could hack her account? She felt a jumble of emotions all at once. She took a deep breath. The fact that he cared enough to dig around to find out about her proved her whole point that there was more between them than he ever admitted. Yet, another part of her felt unsteady, uneasy.

Xavier wouldn't meet her eyes. "Yes," he admitted. "And since you sent a complaint about him, I followed up. I just wanted to make sure you were safe, and I had a bad feeling about that guy so I checked into him. That's when I saw he had a criminal history. That's when I knew I had to warn you."

Emma blinked fast. That was so much information but she could only focus on one thing.

"*You* looked in my account."

First, she felt flattered. He was trying to protect her. Trying to make sure someone followed up on her complaint. Ensuring that she was safe. That felt good.

At the same time, however, she didn't like being in the dark and she felt duped. He'd taken pains to make sure she knew nothing about him, when he knew… everything…down to her billing address and credit card number. "I thought you said knowing things about me would make the sex dull."

Xavier had the decency to look guilty. He raised his hands in surrender. "I'm sorry, Em. I shouldn't have done that, and I know it. I just… I wanted to make sure you were safe and…"

"And you wanted to find out where I lived. Were you just going to pop by sometime? Here I was *not even knowing your name*, and you knew everything about me!" The unfairness of it stung. Also, the mistrust. Did he not trust her to know even the littlest thing about him? Yet, he'd gone and found out everything about her. Without her knowing about it.

Xavier shifted uncertainly on one foot. "Wait," he said, reaching out for her, but she dodged his advance.

"I think you should go home, Xavier," she said, moving away from him. Emma decided she'd go back to Sarah, back to Casey and his friend. Casey might be bland, but he didn't sneak around and find out where she lived behind her back, all while telling her information killed a relationship.

"Emma, please. Let me explain."

"Explain what?" Emma whirled, feeling anger build up in her. "How you lied to me? How you misled me?"

"Let's talk about this."

Emma just felt hurt, betrayed and angry. She didn't want to talk about it. She wanted to go home. "I thought you were honest with me. I thought that's what you said, that strangers could be honest. Be authentic with one another. But you weren't that. You weren't that at all."

That was what hurt the most. Not that he'd snooped, but that he'd kept secrets.

"Emma, if I'd told you the first date that I owned *Nost*, we wouldn't have gotten this far," he said.

"How do you know that?" Emma fired back. "I was honest with you, but you lied to me."

"I just didn't tell you the whole truth," Xavier said, trying to defend himself, raising his voice higher.

"Same thing," she said. "You know what I think? I think this is all about power for you. You want to be the one with all of it. This isn't about love or heartbreak or anything else, it's about you calling all the shots. But that's not how real love works." Emma felt the truth of the words as she said them, understanding for the first time that she'd truly been a pawn in his game. "You told me information would kill the passion in a relationship. Well? You know what, you're right. Knowing this about you. It does kill it."

"Emma!" Xavier exclaimed, pain on his face as if she'd hit him. She felt a flicker of guilt then, but she couldn't let it in. She knew she was right.

"You wanted no strings, right? Well, you got your wish," she said. "There's nothing holding us together." Then she left him.

Xavier watched her go, feeling his gut wrench with guilt and loss. Even worse, he found that she marched right back to her friends, including the decent-looking, but decidedly unremarkable guy who offered her a beer. He felt jealousy well in him, and felt a strong desire to go over there and tell the man to get lost. Who was that? Some other guy on *Nost*, no doubt. The idea of her with another man made his blood boil. *But what claim do I have on her? Everything she told me is true. I lied. I betrayed her trust.*

I was just trying to protect her.

Or was he just trying to keep the balance in the relationship unequal? Was he trying to be the one with all the information? Did he like keeping her in the dark? She accused him of just wanting to keep all the power, and maybe she'd been right. Sure, Sasha had hurt him, more than hurt him, nearly killed him with heartbreak, and maybe he thought the way he'd never let that happen again was just to be sure that he held all the cards. She'd seen right through him, and it scared him to his core.

That was why he'd not revealed who he was at the start. That was why he'd kept all his cards close to his vest.

Yet, the attraction between them was real. Even now, he wanted to sweep Emma off her feet and kiss the life out of her. Even angry, he'd never seen a woman look so beautiful. Her blue eyes flashed fire when they glanced at him, and he wanted to do whatever it took to earn her forgiveness. Did trying to save her from a sexual predator count at all? Would it have been better if he'd just let her take her chances?

Xavier shoved his hands deep in his coat pockets. Should he go after her? Explain himself? He badly wanted to. Then his phone rang. His police detective friend, Ian, was on the line.

"X!" he cried. "It's been too long, buddy." The two of them had gone to school together on the South Side, but now they ran in slightly different circles.

"I know, man, sorry about that. It's been busy."

"Getting all that tail," Ian said.

"Right. That." There was only one bit of tail Xavier wanted at that moment, and she wasn't speaking to him.

"So you got a perp that is getting into your site, huh?" Ian cut right to the chase.

"Anything you can do to help me get him out?" Xavier said. "He's been hassling a…user." The noise in the bar almost made it too hard to hear his friend. Xavier decided to step into the alley to finish the conversation. Getting Cardinals Hat out of his system, and hopefully in jail, was his priority at the moment.

"How bad?" Ian asked, and Xavier filled him in on what had happened so far. Ian made a disappointed sound. "I don't think anything he's done is technically against the law, *but* send me the guy's full name. If he hasn't checked in with his parole officer in a while, that could be enough to lift him, and if you really think he's up to no good, maybe I could get one of my guys to check in on him. See if there's anything to find."

"Could you?" Xavier said, feeling suddenly hopeful.

"Anything for you, X. You know that." Xavier felt suddenly grateful to have such loyal friends.

"Thanks, man."

Something that sounded like a police scanner went off. "We'll have to grab a beer sometime, but right now, I gotta run. City's on fire, as usual."

"Okay, Ian. Thanks, man."

Ian clicked off and Xavier returned to the bar, determined to go find Emma and explain the situation. But when he turned the corner, he found Emma and her friends were already gone.

CHAPTER FIFTEEN

EMMA WENT HOME—alone, after breaking the news to Casey that she wouldn't be his next *Nost* fling. Casey had tried to persuade her, but Emma was in no mood. They'd parted ways as she ducked into her own cab and headed home. Sarah, for her part, had called it an evening early as well, without taking anyone home. The whole mood had turned bleak the second Emma found out Xavier had lied to her. Well, not lied, exactly. Omitted the truth. Still, what an omission.

Emma sat on her bed in the tiny one-bedroom condo and glanced out her window, which overlooked Welles Park. Normally the pretty view of the full trees and big metal gazebo comforted her, but today she just felt isolated and alone. The leaves in the park had turned red and brown in the cool fall night, visible beneath the park's streetlights. Emma sighed, and kicked off her ankle boots, opting to close her shades and then put on a pair of her comfiest flannel pajama bottoms. Emma swept her blond hair up in a messy bun, and grabbed her laptop as she sank into the ruffled pillows on her bed. She felt a storm of different emotions: anger, hurt, but also confusion. She opened up a Word document and did what she always did when she felt this lost: she started to write.

Turns out, the creator of Nost, Xavier Pena, uses it as his own personal playground to pick up unsuspecting women...

Then her fingers froze on the keyboard. Was that fair? Was she being too hard on Xavier? Objectively, what was wrong with the creator of *Nost* using it himself?

He has an unfair advantage for one, and for another, he can secretly look up profile information. The part of her that was still bubbling over with indignation wouldn't be easily appeased.

That was reprehensible, yes, there wasn't a way around that.

Yet, another part of her argued that he wouldn't have stalked her if he hadn't cared. *Why else would he come find me? Warn me about Jimmy?*

Emma stared at the blinking cursor on her computer screen and bit her lip. Was she angry? Sad? Yes, but she wasn't willing to let it all go. Not yet. She'd told Xavier they were done, but in her heart, she knew that wasn't true. And, as much as she hated it, she wasn't done thinking about Xavier.

As if she could conjure him up with just her thoughts, her phone rang. Xavier's number popped up. Surprised, she sent it to voice mail. Then, seconds later, a local number she didn't recognize called. Who was that?

"Hello?"

"It's me. Xavier."

Surprised, she was almost speechless. "You have two phones?"

"The first number… it belongs to a burner phone."

The words hit Emma like a fist. He hadn't trusted her enough to even give her his real number!

"Unbelievable," she murmured.

"Emma… I just want to talk to you. Can we talk? Can I try to explain?"

The sound of his voice still sent reverberations through her stomach. Despite all her best intentions to remain distant and cold, the sound of his voice melted away most of her anger. As she struggled with her feelings, he took that as his opening.

"I'm sorry," he continued, his deep baritone like honey in her ears. Why did even his voice have this effect on her? Why couldn't she just shut off her feelings for him? "I just wanted you to know that. I'm sorry." That was a start, she thought. "I should've told you, but God. This is impossible on the phone. Can I see you?"

Emma glanced down at her flannel PJs. "Uh, no. I don't think that's a good idea."

"I'm on your doorstep. If you want me to go, I will. Just say the word."

In a rush, Emma flew to her living room window and peeked through the curtains. Xavier took a step back and waved up at her. Of course he knew where she lived, she thought. He'd searched through all her *Nost* account information. She felt a renewed surge of anger. How dare he?

"I don't know. Seems like you already know so much about me. You're a stranger, so why would I invite you up?" She watched him on the sidewalk. He looked dejected, in his windbreaker and jeans, his perfectly coifed dark hair seeming to absorb the streetlamp light. He was so tall and imposing in person, and even looking down at him from the third floor, she could see the breadth of his shoulders, see how his big palm dwarfed the cell phone in his hand.

"Emma, I'll tell you whatever you want to know. I swear. Ask me anything."

"Tell me one thing nobody knows about you."

Xavier began to pace on the sidewalk. "What do you mean?"

"A secret. Tell me that, and I'll let you up." She watched him fidget. "Make it a good one."

Xavier bit his lip and let out a long sigh. "Fine." He let out a long breath. "My mom was bipolar. She was institutionalized, too, for a bit when I was young. Only my dad knew about that. I never told anyone. Not even Sasha."

Emma felt blindsided by the sudden revelation. His mother had been bipolar? She realized they had more in common than he thought. Her father suffered from severe depression all his life...and nearly killed himself over it.

"Because of Mom's illness...well, let's just say she had a hard time being faithful to my dad. Not that that stopped him from loving her until the day she died."

"Oh, Xavier," she said, her heart breaking for him. She knew what kind of damage could be wrought between two people who tried to love each other despite their biggest obstacles. Her parents had failed, as her mom made the hard choice to leave her dad when he stopped seeking treatment for his depression.

Xavier glanced up, a pleading look on his face. "Now, will you let me in? Please? It's starting to rain."

Emma glanced at the sidewalk near him and saw it was suddenly dotted with raindrops. He spread his free arm wide.

"Please, Emma. I just want to talk."

Emma considered the request and felt like she couldn't turn him away. Despite feeling betrayed, she still wanted to know more about the man. She couldn't help herself.

She left the window and punched the buzzer, opening the door downstairs. Emma listened to his heavy footsteps on the stairs and then suddenly he was standing at her front door. She'd forgotten at that very moment she was wearing her least sexy pajamas until she looked down. *No matter,* she thought. *Tonight, I'm not getting naked. Not this time. Not before I get some answers.*

Xavier swooped in for a hug but Emma stopped him with her hand.

"You said you wanted to talk," she said, proud of herself for holding him at bay. "That's what we're going to do."

Surprised, Xavier took a step away from her and nodded as he slipped into her living room. "You're right," he agreed. "We should talk."

Emma crossed her arms over her flannel pajama top. "I'm listening."

Xavier sat down on her small leather love seat. "I screwed up, Emma. I know I did. I'm sorry I didn't tell you sooner. What can I do to make it up to you?"

Emma sat down on the small blue chair adjacent to the couch. She didn't trust herself to sit next to him. He already felt too big for her small living room, his long legs nearly bumping against her glass coffee table.

"Tell me about your childhood."

"I don't see how that's relevant." She could see how he took on a defensive stance, his shoulders tensing. He was a walking vault, she thought, a locked door.

"I want to know about you. And you owe me details. That's how you'll make it up to me." Emma crossed her arms across her chest.

Xavier nodded, seeming to get her message: she wanted information and she wanted it now.

"I grew up on the South Side, where most people I knew either grew up to join the police or to join a gang—there really weren't many other options. My dad worked his whole life as a plumber, a decent job, and he was faithful to my mother every day he lived, but..." Xavier shook his head. "She'd go manic sometimes, and when she did that, she was just this unstoppable bundle of energy...and then she'd go out, and sometimes, I don't know why, she just went home with other men. It crushed my father, and I vowed, no matter what, I wouldn't be him."

Emma felt like she began to understand Xavier better. "And then came Sasha."

Xavier nodded. "I was never the get-married type, but I just fell for Sasha hard. I guess she reminded me of my mother in a good way. She wasn't bipolar, wasn't manic, but she had the same kind of charisma, the same energy, I guess. Turns out, they had more in common than I thought. Sasha also cheated when she got bored."

Emma reached out her hand and Xavier took it. She suddenly saw Xavier as he must have felt when he discovered Sasha's infidelity—a scared boy brought right back to when his own mother had done the same to his father. Emma didn't know that. Her mom led a mostly boring life, raising her and her brother in a modest house in the suburbs. They still went home monthly for dinner at Mom's house. Dad moved to California years ago, and they didn't see him much. None of her boyfriends had ever cheated on her—that she knew of. Though, if anything, she'd been tortured with neglect, like with Devin, who'd lost interest the second they'd moved in together.

"Everyone cheats when they get tired of a relationship," Xavier continued.

"I wouldn't." Emma shook her head firmly.

"How do you know?" Xavier cocked his head to one side, doubtful. "Everyone can cheat. Everyone has the capacity to cheat. It's not something you plan, I don't think. It's something...well, you have the need, the resentment builds, and then you find yourself in a stranger's bed."

Emma hesitated. Was that true?

"Ask yourself—if you'd met me in a bar when you were still with Devin... Would you have really turned me down?" A confident smile curved his lips upward. She tried to imagine her life with Devin, if he hadn't taken the job that took him out of state, if she hadn't realized how easy it was to let him go.

"I don't know," she answered honestly. She met his golden gaze and then glanced away, but then studied his thick, strong hands. The hands that she knew could bring her so much pleasure. She shivered. "Maybe," she admitted.

"I know I wouldn't be able to resist you," he said and she felt a growing heat in her belly. He let out a long sigh. "And what if all relationships end that way? All of mine have. Either I've tired of the woman, or the woman has tired of me."

"But..." Frustration welled in Emma. "You can't say for sure *all* relationships are like that. Look, I know many that fail. My parents, for instance."

"What happened with them?" Xavier leaned forward.

"My dad suffered serious depression. He was always switching out meds, but nothing seemed to work. He tried once to kill himself."

"Oh, Emma." Xavier reached out for her hand. She let him take it.

"One day, Dad just decided he'd had enough of the drugs and the therapists, and he just quit. He always said the drugs made him feel like he was sleep-walking through life, and he didn't want to do that anymore, and Mom, well… Mom decided she couldn't handle it anymore. She left him and took us with her."

"I see." Xavier seemed to process this a bit. "So you understand what I mean. Love doesn't last. Your parents were just smart and admitted it earlier than most. Who do you know that's been in a marriage twenty-five years and can't keep their hands off each other?"

Emma thought a second. Aunts and uncles and neighbors flitting through her mind, all couples that seemed decidedly tepid in their affection at best. "I can't, I guess."

"See?" Xavier looked sad. "I don't even know if monogamy is a reasonable goal. For anyone."

Emma felt disappointment strike her fast and hard. She might not be wanting to get married this second, but could Xavier truly feel this way? Was he really so determined never to be faithful?

"It's no accident that *Nost* is so successful. I'm not the only one who feels this way," he said. "I'm not alone.

I made *Nost* because it seemed safe, it seemed like a way to ensure that nobody got close enough to hurt me again. I did it to protect myself, because if I fell for Sasha, I could fall for someone else, and I didn't want to be that vulnerable ever again." Xavier stared at the floor, unable to meet her gaze. Emma saw how vulnerable he was, how open. He looked up then, his golden eyes full of sadness…and something more, guilt. Then it clicked for Emma.

"There wasn't anything wrong with you walking away from Sasha. I know you must feel guilty about that."

Xavier's head snapped up, defensiveness in his posture. "Why do you say that?"

"Because of your father. Your father showed you a model of *always* staying with the person you love, no matter how bad it gets. And you must've felt like maybe…maybe you weren't strong enough to stay with Sasha. But that's not right at all. You stood up for your needs, and that's healthy. That's important. It actually makes you strong, not weak."

"I…" Xavier just stared at her, speechless. "How did you know that? I don't think I've ever really known that. But… You're right. My father, he always seemed so perfect in love, so patient. I'm not that patient. Never was."

"And that's okay. Don't you see?" She squeezed his hand tighter. "Not every relationship is a life sentence. Some don't work out and that's okay, too."

Xavier studied their hands, intertwined. "You make it sound so easy."

"It can be," she urged him.

Xavier leaned forward and gently took her hand in his. "I never thought I'd even consider love again, but you make me wonder. You got past the wall I built, and it was a pretty amazing wall. A hundred feet high, made of steel."

Emma felt her heart surge a little. She had? But did she want that? Xavier was damaged, possibly beyond repair.

"But you don't believe in monogamy."

"That's right." He nodded.

"You think all relationships die."

"Yes."

"So…what are you asking me?" Emma didn't know if she could give him what she wanted. Or that he could give her what she needed.

"I want…to get to know you." The words seemed almost to stick in his throat. "When I'm not with you, I'm thinking about you all the time. I'm Googling you. Hacking the *Nost* database to find out even the smallest detail about you. You intrigue me, Emma Allaire. Even now, wearing that plaid flannel, no makeup on… All I want to do is strip you naked and make you come."

Emma felt warmth creep into her cheeks. All of that was so flattering…and yet, he never wanted a real relationship. He said as much.

"But I thought you didn't want a relationship," she said. "You were so sure."

"I'm not sure I do, and that's just me being honest," Xavier said. "But if I did want one, I'd want one with you."

Xavier moved slowly closer to her, leaned in so their knees touched. Emma felt a spark even through her flannel bottoms. Why did the proximity of this man do such things to her? She knew she ought to keep her guard up and yet, all she wanted to do right then was lean forward and put her mouth on his.

"Be honest with me, Emma. Do you even know what you want? You had experience before me, but that experience…well…" He grinned. "You've had boyfriends who've never pleasured you the way I have."

This was a true statement.

"Do you want to explore this chemistry? You and I both know this doesn't come along every day. Do you really want to end it?" That had been *her* argument, and now he'd co-opted it. Xavier was now firmly in her personal space. She could smell his scent: something spicy and sweet. No, she didn't want to end it. Not really. That had been a lie.

He leaned forward and whispered in her ear, "Say the word, and I'll go."

"I—I don't want you to go." Her voice was a low croak.

"Then, come here." His voice left no room for argument as he patted his own lap. She slid off her chair and went to him, her body seeming to have a mind of its own. She straddled him on her sofa, distantly realizing her curtains beyond were slightly parted. *This is more privacy than an alley,* she reasoned, but somehow, with Xavier, she still felt on display. It was the way he looked at her, drinking her in.

He tackled the buttons of her pajama top one by one, each one releasing a bit more skin, as she stared at him. Now that she knew more about him, about his difficult childhood, all she wanted to do was comfort him, make it better, heal those old wounds. Knowing more about him made her fiercely protective, too. *I want to fix you,* she thought in her head, as he slid her top free. Naked beneath, she arched her back a bit, her nipples puckering in the cool air of her condo. He murmured his appreciation as he rubbed one nipple with his finger, and cupped the other breast with his hand.

"You're beautiful," he said, studying her body. "Simple perfection."

His gentle touch sent ripples of pleasure through her body as she leaned into his touch. She could feel his lap stiffen in anticipation, and she ground into him as she bent down and claimed his mouth with hers. The fireworks began then, passion exploding in her mind with urgent want. Knowing him made the kiss even *more* intense, she thought, as she anticipated every move his mouth made. She knew him on a deeper level and that made the passion even stronger. Couldn't he feel that, she wondered? Couldn't he feel how well their mouths fit together?

Xavier broke free. "I want you," he murmured.

"I want you, too," she replied, a low whisper in her throat.

Then Xavier stood, lifting her in his arms, as if she weighed nothing. He carried her to her bedroom, where he laid her gently on her bed and kissed her once more, their tongues melting together in a desperate heat. Here, with his weight on her chest, she felt like she'd known him for years. He anticipated her every want, his hands driving her wild. He seemed to know exactly how she wanted to be touched, as if he could see right into her mind. She let him take her to the places she knew he would, leading her right to the edge.

Xavier devoured Emma's body. He couldn't get enough of her, her perfectly puckered pink nipples, the way she moaned in such delight as he touched her. Her body was an instrument he'd never get tired of playing, and as he explored her curves, he realized with a shock that he'd never felt this way about anyone before. Was it her amazing pheromones? She smelled delicious, and tasted even better. He'd had many women, but something about her just instantly made him hard. His desire and need for her thrilled him and frightened him all at once. If he needed her this badly, what would happen when he lost her?

He tried to push the worry from his mind, even as he slipped inside her, feeling her tense around him, hugging him so deliciously tight. She wrapped her bare legs around his waist and he thought he might come then and there. Amazing. Just absolutely amazing. Mind-blowing, even. Could he allow himself the risk of wanting her? Did he even have a choice?

She pulled him deeper inside her, and he knew he wouldn't be able to last much longer. He needed to fill her, needed to make her his.

CHAPTER SIXTEEN

XAVIER CAME AWAKE the next morning to the smell of pancakes filling the small apartment. He rolled over and found Emma's side of the bed empty, and heard the clatter in the kitchen that was his lover making him breakfast. He fell back into his pillow, inhaling the sweet scent, feeling strangely satisfied. Perhaps it was because he'd spent the night exploring Emma's body. God, he just never got tired of the woman. Could it be that they shared a passion that wouldn't wane?

He sat up on his elbows. He still wasn't convinced. He wasn't like his father. He didn't believe that love came to stay. He believed that love came and went, on its own accord, on a timetable known to no one. He was playing with fire with Emma, and he knew it. He shouldn't have spent the night, shouldn't have indulged in all that sex. He felt warm and comfortable, and that was dangerous. He grabbed his phone off the dresser and glanced at the face of it. No urgent messages from work, so he had that flexibility. He noticed the *Nost* app told him he had ten messages waiting for him, but for once, he didn't feel the urge to check them. He remembered, distantly, messaging a few women last night before he discovered that Emma might be in trouble. Now that urge to see another woman faded into the background. He had all the woman he wanted, right here. Of course, that was what troubled him. He still felt uneasy about his growing need for Emma. The lazy Sunday stretched out before him and all he wanted to do was spend it with Emma. Preferably naked.

He rolled from bed, pulled up his boxers and his jeans and walked into the living room. He saw Emma, blond hair messy, wearing an oversized sweatshirt and nothing else, and he wanted to spend the day with her. Hell, the month. Maybe longer.

"Morning, sexy," Emma called from the kitchen, her eyes flicking appreciatively down his bare chest. "You hungry?"

"Starved." He grinned as he set his phone on the breakfast bar. "We worked up an appetite."

"You bet we did." Emma sent him a knowing glance and her delicate features made his groin tighten. God, she was beautiful. What had he done to deserve such a beautiful woman? He wanted to drop at her feet and worship her…with his tongue, he thought, a wry smile spreading across his face. He closed the distance between them and swept her into his arms, dipping his head so he could kiss her lips. Her lips were so willing, so soft, that he wasn't sure if he could control himself long enough to eat breakfast.

Emma fed him a bite of pancake.

"Mmm, delicious," he said, appreciative, as she flipped the last pancake onto a nearby plate. He grabbed the syrup from the table and the bowl of berries she'd washed and headed to her breakfast bar.

"I'll get a separate plate," she offered, but he waved her off.

"Let's share one," he said.

She giggled and then took the tall stack of pancakes to the bar. The coffeemaker dinged, announcing a new full pot of coffee. "Do you want coffee?" she asked him. "Do you even…drink coffee?"

"I do. Black," he said.

"Oh, too strong for me," she said, grinning, as she poured her own cup and added a hefty serving of milk so that the cup was almost beige and three big spoonfuls of sugar. "I like it sweet." He found, with surprise, that he liked that little detail. Now he knew how she took her coffee. Wasn't that something every long-term couple knew? Usually those kinds of details made him nervous, but suddenly, he was glad to store that bit away. Remember it for later. He wondered what would be her favorite order from Starbucks. He found himself wanting to know more about her, that no detail seemed too small. *What was happening to me?*

"Syrup?" he asked her, and she nodded.

"Yes, please. As much as you can handle. Sweet tooth, can you tell?" She grinned at him. He doused the stack in syrup and then took a hunk of the stack and offered it to her. She leaned in and took the bite, as he watched her perfectly pink lips wrap around the fork.

"Mmmmmm," she murmured, closing her eyes. "Delicious."

"Not as delicious as you," he said and grabbed a bite for himself. "What's your favorite meal of the day?"

"Breakfast, by far," she answered immediately.

"Have you been to Dawn? The new restaurant in the west Loop?"

Emma shook her head.

"I have to take you there," he said. "You're going to love it. They have this amazing banana walnut French toast." Xavier found himself eager to take her to his new favorite brunch place, as soon as possible...maybe even next weekend. The fact that he was already making plans in his head with Emma for the following week should've caused him more anxiety, but instead it all just felt right. He'd take Emma out next Sunday, because he'd see her that whole weekend. He'd make sure of it.

"I'd love to go." She took another bite of pancake and he felt buoyant, upbeat.

"What do you want to do today?" he asked her. "Go out? Stay in?" He pushed his knee against hers.

"Anything you want to do," she said. "I've got no plans."

"Let's play it by ear."

Soon enough, the two polished off their plate of pancakes, Xavier feeling happily full. Usually, he watched his carb and sugar intake. You couldn't get cut muscles on a diet of junk, but even he had his splurge days. Today would be one of them, he decided. He went into the bedroom to grab his shirt, the air in the apartment suddenly feeling chilly.

He helped Emma clean up the dishes and then he joined her on the couch. She flicked on the TV and he joined her, as the political shows came on.

"I always watch," Emma said, nodding to the roundtable commentators on the screen. "I like to know what's going on."

"Me, too," Xavier said, surprised to find someone else who was interested in politics. Usually, reality TV took a front seat and news a backseat. *Everything I learn about her just makes me love her more.* The thought shocked even him. Was he really thinking about *love*?

They settled in to watch the show and Emma curled up next to him, and the feel of her cuddled under his arm made everything feel right in the world. She pulled up a soft throw and tucked it around them. They just fit together, like they were made for each other. Their passion was amazing, that was true, and yet, here, in this tender moment, Xavier felt content as well. Could they really have both passion and tenderness? Was that even possible? Normally, Xavier felt restless when he sat with a woman—he usually only felt at home when the clothes were off—but here, snuggled in together on a couch beneath a blanket, he felt like there was nowhere else he wanted to be. The restlessness in him evaporated. He could see himself here, on her couch, with her in his arms, watching TV for endless weekends to come.

Was he really settling in? Was he really considering a serious relationship?

Something about Emma just made the whole idea seem not just possible, but inevitable. They fit together in a way he'd never fit with another woman. Could he take the chance that maybe he'd been wrong about relationships? Emma snuggled into him and he felt happy. How could he *not* take the chance? He wanted this: Emma in his arms, naked and wild on Saturday night, and then tender and cuddly Sunday morning. Maybe he could have both. Maybe he should try.

During a commercial break, Emma shifted a bit against him, and Xavier stretched, too.

"Nature's calling," he said, hating to break their warm embrace. "I'll be right back."

Emma watched Xavier dip into the adjacent bathroom and sighed. She could get used to that amazing hunk of man walking around her apartment. She hadn't realized how small it was before she saw his broad shoulders in it, seemingly taking up all the available space. She didn't mind, though. He was tall and imposing, and, oh, so strong. She thought back to how he'd picked her up the night before and carted her off to the bedroom, and she could feel the tingle of the memory in her toes. She still wasn't sure how she felt about his relationship anxiety, the way he seemed so skittish about commitment. She told herself she wasn't exactly looking for a ring on her finger either at the moment, but since she'd never had a casual one-night stand, she didn't know exactly how to do casual. All she knew at that moment was that Xavier made her knees weak, and she wanted more of him. Much more.

She knew how he took his coffee, and that he liked watching news shows, just like she did. They had so much in common, and yet there was so much she still didn't know about him.

Emma snuggled up on the couch with the blanket just as his phone sitting on the coffee table dinged. She recognized the sound: it was an incoming message from *Nost.* Emma glanced up at the closed bathroom door. Should she snoop? No. She knew she shouldn't. That was wrong. And yet... She couldn't fight the thirst for curiosity about this man. She wanted to know everything about him. Curiosity overcame her at that very moment. She pushed down the blanket and glanced at the phone, which was still lit with the new message.

Hey sexy. Let's get naked tonight.

The message sent a chill through her. A pit formed in her stomach. Now, unable to contain herself, she grabbed the phone and touched the message and his *Nost* app came up. The message was from a gorgeous brunette who wasn't afraid to use a string bikini shot as her profile picture. She was all cleavage and amazingly flat stomach, a little hoop through her belly button.

She was blowing a kiss to the camera. Emma couldn't help herself then. She swiped through other messages. Xavier had dozens, and that was just in the last twenty-four hours. He'd also reached out to a few on his own just last night. *Last night.* Right before he texted her, he'd texted three other girls. With the clear intent to meet them. Emma bit her lip.

The betrayal hit her hard. Had he only reached out to her because the others hadn't responded quickly enough?

She felt the pit in her stomach grow bigger. Jealousy flared in her, taut and ugly, and yet she knew logically she had no reason to be jealous. He'd been up front with her, hadn't he? He'd told her he had no intention of being monogamous. He was the *founder* of *Nost.* Why wouldn't he still be using the app? Yet, all the gorgeous women, some even younger than her, made her feel nauseous suddenly. This was what Xavier's life was like: a phone full of beautiful women ready to take their clothes off for him, and he was only too happy to oblige them. She thought of her face in the roster, just one more in a never-ending list of conquests.

The room spun. *I can't do this,* Emma thought, panic in her throat. *I just can't.*

"Emma? What are you doing?" Xavier had come out of the bathroom and stood hesitantly outside the door.

Emma was caught, his phone in her hand. And she felt awash with another wave of new emotions: shame, guilt, embarrassment. She'd been caught snooping. Yet, now, she couldn't unsee what she saw. She wished she'd never looked at his phone. It was one thing to imagine him with other women. It was another thing to see their faces.

"I think you should go," Emma said, handing him his phone and wrapping the blanket tightly around her.

Confusion flickered across his face. "Emma… what?" Xavier took the phone reluctantly. He glanced down and saw the *Nost* app open. "Emma, you can't be mad about this. You know I'm not looking for anything exclusive. I thought… I mean, we talked about this."

"I know we did," Emma said, nodding, biting her lip to fight back the tears that threatened to spill. *I was just one woman among so many. He never cared about me. He isn't capable of caring about any one woman.* "I thought I could do it, but I can't."

Xavier moved forward, ready to join her on the couch. Emma, in a panic, stood, dropping the blanket on the floor.

"No," she said, shaking her head and wrapping her arms around herself. "I thought I could do casual. I just can't. I can't. The idea of you being with me and then all those other women…" She stared at his phone. "It makes me sick to my stomach. I thought I could do breezy and cool, but you know what? That's just not me."

Xavier stood, sadness stooping his shoulders. "You shouldn't have looked on my phone."

"I know." Emma hugged herself even tighter, wishing she could take back the last five minutes, wishing she'd played it differently. But, then again, didn't she *need* to know?

"Why did you?"

"Because…because… I want to know. Everything about you. I guess."

"Now you know." Xavier glanced at the *Nost* app and frowned. "But I told you…this is who I am. I can't do commitment. I can barely even do more than a one-night stand. I told you."

"I know you did." Emma bit her lip, the tears forming a lump in her throat. He had been honest with her. It's not like he'd tried to hide his proclivities. "I thought I could do this. Imagining you with another woman… it hurts."

Now is the time for you to tell me that you'll change, Emma thought. *Now's the time to tell me that those women don't mean anything to you, that you're ready to take a chance on us.*

But when she looked up at him, Xavier stared at her helplessly. He seemed unable to give her what she wanted.

The two stood in silence for a moment, the weight of the impasse building an invisible wall between them.

Emma took a deep breath and tried to muster the courage to ask him the question she needed to ask, but was suddenly afraid of his answer.

"Would you have slept with one of those women last night if we hadn't met?"

Xavier glanced at the floor. "Yes," he admitted.

The admission hit her hard. It almost felt like a physical blow to her stomach, a deep jab. She took a step backward. She had no right to feel this hurt. He'd told her what he wanted, told her who he was, and yet, she couldn't deny the pain, the hurt, of realizing she was just a cog in a wheel, one more body among dozens.

Why couldn't she be enough? It was the question that bounced around her head, and made her feel small and insignificant.

"Would you ever not do that? Would you ever consider quitting *Nost*?"

Xavier ran a hand through his thick, jet-black hair. "Emma, I told you—"

"Yes, yes, I know. You're afraid of love. Of risking anything. You'd rather..." Emma bit back her words. She couldn't say them out loud. *You'd rather sleep with a new woman every day.*

Xavier took another step closer. "You knew this about me, Emma. I told you the very first day." Xavier reached up to hold her, but Emma jumped back.

"I know you did." She didn't want him touching her. Didn't want to melt back into his embrace and have all logic fly out the window. She didn't want to turn a blind eye to this, to pretend it was all okay with her. Because it wasn't.

"You seemed to be willing to try..." Xavier paused, seeming to have trouble putting a label on whatever it was they were trying.

He was right. She had been willing last night to invite him into her bed. He'd not made any promises, really. He hadn't even said he wanted a relationship, exactly, only that he'd been drawn to her, intrigued by her. That had been enough last night for her to wiggle out of her panties, but now in the gray light of morning, with his phone dinging with incoming messages from strange women, it just didn't seem enough.

"I guess I was wrong." Emma couldn't look him in the eye. She wanted him to tell her that those other women didn't mean anything, that he could quit them anytime he wanted to, but the longer he stood there without saying those words, the more she came to be convinced that they mattered to him more than she did. "If you can't… I mean, if you have to keep seeing other women while you see me, then I can't do this."

"Emma." Xavier let out a long breath. "I just…don't know if I can do that."

"Would you even try, though? That's what I want to know." Emma met his eyes and saw the conflicting emotions there, and the conflict within him hurt her even more. Why didn't she mean enough to him to even say he'd *try*? She knew what they had was special, so why didn't he?

"Emma, what are you asking me to do? Not see anyone else?"

Emma nodded.

His phone dinged with another incoming message from *Nost*, another woman looking to have sex with him.

"Would you tell her, that one, right now, that you're

not interested?" Emma pointed to his phone. He looked at it and then back at her. He hesitated too long. Now, whatever he said, she thought, might be a lie. "You need to go."

"Emma, come on. Let's talk about this."

Emma shook her head, the tears threatening to spill, and the last thing she wanted was for him to see her cry.

"Now," she said, marching to the door and opening it. Now would be the time for Xavier to tell her he'd try. That he didn't care about the women on his phone, that all he ever wanted was her. But, instead, he just grabbed his jacket and wallet from the chair in her living room and headed out. She didn't know what hurt more: the fact that he'd probably go right on out and meet one of his *Nost* conquests or that he left without a single backward glance.

CHAPTER SEVENTEEN

XAVIER SAT ON the Brown Line train, which would take him to the Loop, which would mean a quick walk to his condo. The cityscape rushed by outside, a blur of brownstone buildings out his window on the elevated train tracks, as they weaved through buildings toward the Fullerton stop. He thought of the look of hurt and betrayal on Emma's face and her eyes glassy with unshed tears as he left her apartment and couldn't help but feel a pang of guilt. Yet, why was he the one feeling guilty? He'd been honest about who he was. He didn't try to hide or lie about anything, and she still ended up hurt anyway.

He shook his head as he stared out the train's window. He should've known the very night he met her that this was a mistake. He knew she'd never done this before, had even been reluctant about trying it, and so he ought to have known she couldn't handle it. Xavier sat down and scrolled through his *Nost* app. It was probably for the best. She'd ended what he couldn't, and it would've just led to disaster anyway. Relationships didn't work. *Just ask Sasha.*

The train rattled to a stop and a few passengers got off. Then a sexy blonde got on. She wore knee-high black boots with stiletto heels, skintight leggings and a short black leather jacket. Xavier couldn't help but notice her as she slid down into a seat across from him on the train. She wore heavy smoky makeup and looked like she was headed out somewhere, even though it was only midafternoon. She made eye contact with him, her blue eyes serious in a look that told Xavier she was at minimum not disinterested. He hadn't shaved, and wore his clothes from last night, but there was no mistaking the fact that she'd noticed him. Then she dug out her phone. Seconds later, his own dinged with an incoming message.

He picked it out of his pocket and saw that the slinky blonde across from him had just sent him a message on *Nosi*.

What's a fine man like you doing on the Brown Line? She'd written.

When he glanced up, there was no mistaking the look on her face: desire, interest, a decided invitation. *It has to be a sign,* he thought, a sign that he should try to forget Emma as soon as possible. Xavier smiled at the woman, and she grinned back.

Well, well, well. The universe just delivered a sign that he couldn't ignore.

Emma met Sarah that afternoon for a late lunch in Lincoln Square. The small Greek restaurant was half-full, despite the odd hour, though outside the weather had turned decidedly colder and the gray sky matched Emma's gloomy mood. Fall had arrived, and Emma sat at the table wearing an oversized scarf around her neck, still fighting off the chill outside despite having been inside for fifteen minutes. Then again, she felt like she hadn't been able to get warm since Xavier left her place that morning. She wondered if she'd ever see him again.

Emma had told Sarah the whole story, ending with Xavier's abrupt departure.

"It's all my fault," Sarah said. "I never should've turned you on to *Nost*. I knew you couldn't handle it."

"Exactly! This *is* all your fault," Emma moaned, but she didn't mean it, not really. "No, it's not, Sarah. You were just trying to get me laid."

"Well, at least you were successful there."

Emma sighed and rolled her eyes. "Too successful, actually. He was *so* good, though. In bed. He said it was because we were strangers, but do you buy that?"

Sarah considered this a moment, her fork paused over the salad she'd ordered. "Maybe. Sometimes. Rarely, actually. I mean, stranger sex can be great but it's always going to be on the surface. Like simply scratching an itch." Sarah took a bite of salad and nibbled. "Look, I love a good one-night stand, but nothing beats really knowing a person. The best orgasms happen after you drop the L-bomb."

Emma raised a skeptical eyebrow. "You've told someone you've loved them? When?"

"College." Sarah shrugged and pushed the salad around on her plate. "Since then, I haven't found anybody else worthy."

Emma laughed. The hamburger that sat before her was largely untouched. She'd thought she wanted comfort food, but now, faced with it, she'd lost her appetite. She worried it had everything to do with Xavier. "Still, the queen of *Nost* believes in love."

"Sure I do. It's what we all want, isn't it?"

Emma picked up a French fry and chewed on it absently. "All of us except Xavier."

Sarah shook her head as she took a sip of her water. "I still can't believe the guy *started* the app. I mean, he must be a bizillionaire."

"Who knows? I don't even know where he lives." Or much else about him either. Except how he takes his coffee, and *the way he sounds when he comes*. The dirty thought popped into her head unbidden. Damn that man. Every time she thought of him, she felt a little tingle down the back of her legs.

"Oh, that would be easy to find with property records. I could look that up for you in a second."

Emma nibbled on another fry, chewing thoughtfully. "I'm almost tempted."

"It would only be mildly stalkerish," Sarah said.

Emma shook her head. "No. Not going to do it. He's a toxic bachelor, he admits it. Why would I want to get involved in that?"

"Because you already are," Sarah pointed out. "I can tell this is bothering you. Hitting you hard."

"I know!" Emma sank her head into her hands. "But why? We've only had sex a couple of times, and... I mean, I knew what I was getting into... But..."

"He's got a magic penis. Made of crack?"

Emma barked a laugh. "Kind of."

"Makes you do things you'd never do, and now you're addicted." Sarah wiped her mouth with her napkin, sounding as if she'd run into a crack penis before.

Emma nodded. "But I just *can't* do this casual thing. I tried, but the second I saw those other messages on his phone..."

"You felt like shit," Sarah finished as Emma sighed.

"Exactly. You should have seen him, Sarah. He was all, 'I told you about this.' He's never going to change. I can see it on his face. All those articles I read about commitment-phobes said the only cure is them *wanting* to change. Nothing else will help. And he doesn't want to."

Sarah gave a half shrug. "Leopards and spots. But I'll tell you one thing. If he doesn't realize how amazing you are, then let him go."

Emma felt weighed down and sad. She still didn't understand how such a quick relationship could affect her so deeply. She even had trouble explaining it to her best friend, but it all had to do with a feeling that their connection meant more, that somehow it was special, even if Xavier refused to see it.

"I don't know if it'll be that easy."

Sarah reached out and patted her friend's hand. "Well, I'm proud of you. You stuck to your boundaries, you know? You didn't cave. Casual isn't what you want, and so you kicked him out of your place. I don't know if I would've been able to do that."

"Oh, sure you would."

Sarah shrugged. "Nah. You're so good at not taking shit from people. Love that you're not afraid to ask for what you want."

Emma smiled weakly at her friend. "Except that Xavier's not going to give it to me."

"Who knows?" Sarah said, waving her fork in the air. "He might come around yet. You're an amazing woman, and if he doesn't see that, *he's* the fool. I don't care how good-looking or rich he is."

"I hope you're right." Emma couldn't shake the sinking feeling that no matter what, Xavier wouldn't change. He'd warned her, after all. She remembered the look of resignation as he left her apartment earlier that morning. He was stuck in his ways and not about to change, for her or anyone else.

The waiter came with the bill and Sarah snatched it out of his hand. "I'm getting this," she said. "Least I can do since I caused all this drama."

Emma laughed. "I agree with that. You are totally paying for this," she joked.

Back at her condo, Emma started working on a new story for her editor, but no matter how she tried to write a follow-up to her first Mr. X story, she just couldn't seem to finish this one. With a jolt, she realized that part of the reason she had trouble writing was that writing about it made it all final, somehow, and she wasn't ready for that. Emma abandoned her Word document, with only two paragraphs written and a blinking cursor silently admonishing her that she'd need at least 800 more words to sell her editor. Instead, she pulled up a browser and typed *Xavier Pena* into Google.

Dozens of articles popped up about him being a tech prodigy, a cutting-edge app developer whose future was bright. Tinder had offered to buy him out, and reportedly at a hefty multimillion-dollar payout, though he'd yet to accept their offer or anyone else's. Sarah was right about his bank account at least. Xavier's social media accounts came up then and she clicked on them, finding them strangely bare of personal information. She expected to see an account full of selfies with beautiful, willing fans, but instead, she found hardly anything posted by the *Nost* creator. His accounts, Instagram and Facebook were thin, with hardly any posts, and those that were there largely centered around *Nost* milestones and his dad, though a quick look through Instagram found a picture of a funeral, a snapshot of his father's picture in front of a ring of memorial flowers. His father died a year ago.

He hadn't mentioned that.

She dug deeper to find an obituary to find out why he'd died. She read the small notice:

Henri Pena died of a heart attack. His wife, Gena, died eighteen years before. She struggled with bipolar disorder. Pena never remarried, citing Gena as the love of his life. He is survived by a son, Xavier...

Emma stared at the article online. Xavier lost his father a year ago. Then he lost his fiancé. The emotional trauma went much deeper than she realized.

Not exactly going to convince him that trying love again is a good idea.

Emma sighed. No wonder he didn't want to risk a relationship. She stared at Xavier's picture, wondering how she could convince him to try, and yet she knew it was out of her hands. He had to decide to risk his heart and his future. There was nothing she could do.

Emma pulled up her Word document once more and began typing.

The mystery woman from the subway train led Xavier by the hand to the steps of her apartment building and with a quick punch of numbers on a keypad, buzzed them both inside. On the stairwell, she turned and pressed her body against his, so that he felt the fullness of her breasts, even through her leather jacket, and even without kissing him, she reached up and gently massaged his groin, a bold, aggressive move that would normally have him standing at attention inside of a minute. But for some reason her touch felt clumsy and awkward, and he was keenly aware of her too-red lipstick. Everything about her was just…wrong. Not that she wasn't gorgeous—the woman could have any man she wanted, especially with that body—but there was something about her that was just lacking.

Xavier realized it was because she wasn't Emma.

Every time he looked at this mystery woman all he could think was: *her nose isn't as cute as Emma's. Her hands are bigger than Emma's. Her butt's almost too skinny. Not like Emma's.* No matter how hard he tried, he couldn't shut his brain off. She went on working him with her hand, but she was quickly finding him unresponsive. Would he not even be able to get hard?

That had never happened to Xavier before. Not once. *This woman before you is gorgeous. What's your problem?* A voice shouted in his head. But he knew exactly what his problem was: Emma.

"Kiss me," she murmured, flicking her hair back, too-red lips parted. Xavier didn't want to. That was the worst part. This woman was willing and sexy and he...didn't want to kiss her. Yet, he dipped his head and kissed her anyway. She slipped her tongue in his mouth, and ground against him. Every move she made just made him less turned on. Because she wasn't Emma.

When you fall in love, other women, they just aren't as beautiful, his father had told him. Xavier never believed him. Now, he wasn't so sure. He thought he'd loved Sasha, but he'd always been able to look at other women, appreciate them. Now, here with this woman from the train, objectively gorgeous, he couldn't even appreciate how sexy she was.

"Come on," the woman said, taking his hand and leading him down to the basement apartment—her apartment. Part of him wanted to flee. What was he doing here? He should go find Emma. Apologize, try to convince her that he'd been wrong.

Had he? Was he really going to turn Nost off? What would his co-workers say, what would the investors say? The headline: *Founder finds true love on No Strings website* didn't seem like it would exactly reel in users.

He followed the woman down the stairs and into her apartment as the door shut behind them. Yet, was he really going to do this? He glanced around at the woman's mismatched furniture, the clutter of junk mail choking the coffee table, an empty pizza box sitting on the kitchen counter. The apartment was nothing like Emma's carefully designed place, where every piece of furniture seemed made for the space, where she had her pots and pans neatly hanging from a rack above her sink. He could relax there all day. But here? No. Here would be a quick and dirty fuck and then he'd never see this apartment again. Or this woman. And he'd never know her name, either.

Normally, the idea of that turned him on, made him so hard he could feel the blood pulsating to his very tip, but that was before Emma. The thought of Emma made him want to go be with her. Made him want to see if she could rouse him where this woman couldn't.

Now would be the time that Xavier would normally

pounce, where he'd work his magic on a stranger, but instead, he just stood in her living room feeling uncertain.

"What you say we get our freak on, Mr. X?" she said, and her words jarred him back to reality. She grabbed his crotch once more, but it didn't respond to her touch. The strange woman didn't seem to care. She knelt before him and began to unzip his pants.

"How about I suck on you awhile?"

The idea of this woman doing that…well, he just knew it wouldn't work. Knew he wouldn't get hard.

"Wait," he said, stopping her. He couldn't believe he was doing this. He'd never turned down an offer like this before. Had he gone mad?

No, he could almost hear his father say. *No, you're just falling in love. Love is its own kind of madness.*

"Mr. X? Something wrong, sugar?" she asked him, as he pulled away from her. She pulled herself to her feet.

"I just… I'm sorry. I can't do this." He ran a hand through his hair while the woman just stared at him.

"Newbie, huh?" She crossed her arms across her chest, every move now skeptical. Apparently, she'd run into reluctant men on *Nost* before. That surprised Xavier. He hadn't realized men would be reticent. Not with a woman as gorgeous as this one in front of him. "Or married?" She quirked an eyebrow.

"Newbie," he lied. New to love, though, so it wasn't all a lie. He zipped his pants and backed out of her apartment, glancing back once at the disapproving look on the train girl's face. "It's not you," he said.

"Oh, hell, honey, I *know* it's not me." She sat on her sofa and crossed her fit legs, showing a flash of inner thigh. She shook her head as if to say, *you're missing out,* and part of him knew he was. Even as Xavier left, gently shutting the apartment door behind him, he still couldn't believe he was doing this. He never thought he'd ever feel about a woman the way he felt about Emma. Sure, he'd loved Sasha, but if a gorgeous woman had been on her knees offering him a little piece of heaven, he seriously doubted he'd be able to resist. Emma was different. Emma consumed his thoughts, made him want to be a better man. That was it, really. He'd need to try to be the man Emma deserved.

He flagged down the nearest cab.

All he wanted to do now was find Emma.

CHAPTER EIGHTEEN

On her way home from lunch, Emma made a few stops including the corner grocery store where she grabbed a few essentials for the week. Her hands laden with a couple of bags, she still felt a heavy weight on her shoulders as she thought about Xavier. She didn't know why he'd gotten to her so much, but then she knew why: she'd fallen for him. It was that simple. Sarah was right. He did have a magic penis, but he had more than that. She just felt she *got* him on a deeper level. She understood what it was like to grow up with two very dysfunctional parents as they tried to navigate the ups and downs of serious issues. As much as she wanted to make it just about the sex, it wasn't. If her own mother had stayed with her chronically depressed father she might have turned out just like Xavier: feeling that no matter what, love was a life sentence.

No wonder he was so riddled with relationship anxiety, unable to commit on the most basic level. But maybe she ought to let him go. After all, he didn't seem all that willing to change his ways. She remembered the expression on his face when she asked him about ever quitting *Nost*. His answer was plain to see: never. He was probably, right at that moment, texting another woman, figuring out a time to meet. Then she'd only know him as Mr. X. The thought sent a spike of jealousy into her brain, like an icicle, cold and unyielding. She hated that feeling.

The cold fall wind sliced through her thin utility jacket as she walked down the leaf-laden street near her condo. The sidewalk was surprisingly empty for a Sunday afternoon, and Emma figured the gloom and dark clouds above that threatened rain kept everyone inside. She felt a cold drop on her cheek and hurried her pace, hoping to make it to her condo before the rain hit.

Her phone dinged with the telltale sound announcing an incoming message from *Nost,* and she paused on the street. She'd forgotten she'd even had the app running at all, and made a mental note to delete it. After all, what was the point in being on it? She'd proven to herself that casual wasn't what she wanted, and the idea of floating around in the universe that Xavier created felt too painful suddenly.

She shifted the bags in her arms so that her right held them both, and then fished her phone out of her pocket.

Her heart lifted a bit. Maybe Xavier had texted her? Maybe he'd changed his mind? But why would he use *Nost*? He had her number.

Then she pulled up the message, from a handle she didn't recognize: *Cuming4U.*

Ugh, how cheesy, she thought, as she flipped open the message. She nearly stopped in her tracks. *Cuming4U* had the photo of the man in the Cardinals hat. He wasn't even trying to hide behind a fake photo anymore. *Here he was.* She clicked the link to read the full message.

Those bags look heavy. Want some help?

Goose bumps stood up on the back of her neck. Frantically, she glanced around her. Where was he? All she saw was a younger woman walking her dog across the street, and only one other couple walking away from her ahead on the sidewalk, hand in hand. No cars pulled by on the small side street, either. Where was he? She glanced at nearby condo windows, but saw no one. Still, she could almost feel his eyes on her, watching every move she made. Her own condo was more than a block away. Was he following her? How had he even found her? Was it just luck…or something more sinister?

She fumbled with her phone, trying to turn off her location setting, but even as she did so, she knew it was too late. In her haste, she dropped one of her grocery bags and an apple rolled out.

"Dammit," she cursed, stooping to pick up her groceries.

Another message from *Nost* dinged.

Love it when you bend over.

Now she just wanted to quit the app. She wanted him out of her phone, out of her life. She picked up the apple, shoved it into her bag and whipped the reusable tote over her shoulder. Another message followed.

Better watch it, or the apple isn't the only thing that's going to get bruised.

In a panic, Emma deleted the entire app off her phone. Her heart thudded in her chest as she frantically scanned her surroundings. Now it was just the woman walking the dog, who'd gone halfway down the block. The couple had turned at the corner, and the street was empty save for a few parked cars. Where was he? How was he watching her? She quickened her pace to her apartment, wondering what she should do: Call the police? They might laugh at her. What would she say? A mean guy is texting me? Claiming to be watching me?

Yet, the hairs on her forearms stood straight up. She knew with certainty that the man was nearby somewhere, and she knew he planned to hurt her. She remembered Xavier saying the man had a record, a history of assaulting women. She didn't know what to do, so she called Xavier. The phone rang once before he picked it up.

"Emma. I'm so glad you called, I..."

"Xavier. He's here. The guy who wore the Cardinals hat. Somehow he found me, but I don't know how. He's been messaging me and I think he's watching me. Can you talk to me while I get to my apartment? I'm just a half block away now."

"Emma, you need to call 911. Now." Xavier sounded panicked. "Get inside your apartment as fast as you can. I'm coming to you now. I'll be there as fast as I can."

Her heart thudded even faster as she threw a quick glance behind her. Still no sign of the man, but she knew he was watching her. She could feel it.

"Are you sure?"

"More than sure. Hang up. Now. Call 911."

"Okay," she agreed, suddenly even more afraid than she was before. She'd never heard Xavier sound so rattled. The fact that she wasn't overreacting to the situation didn't make her feel any better. Reluctantly, she hung up. Emma quickened her pace so that she was almost jogging as she headed to the stoop of her three-flat, which she could see. It was just about fifteen feet away. Emma fumbled with her phone, dialing *9-1-1.* She was about to hit send when she felt someone come up behind her. Then came the rough hand that slapped her arm and her phone went flying. She whirled in time to see the man she'd dreaded. He wasn't wearing his Cardinals hat now, but she'd recognize the cold glint of his gaze anywhere.

"Where you going so fast, Kitten?" he said, voice low and full of menace.

Xavier's heart leapt to his throat as he began his full-on sprint from the Brown Line L stop near Emma's condo.

He'd already dialed his Chicago detective friend, Ian, who happened to be on duty not far away.

"I'll be there in five minutes," Ian said, and he could hear the whir of the siren of his unmarked police car in the background as he flicked it on.

"I'll be there in two," Xavier said, kicking it up a notch as he ran even faster, his arms pumping, his heart beating wildly in his chest.

Please let her be okay, he prayed. *If that asshole so much as touches her, I'm going to kill him,* he vowed as he skidded to the corner of Emma's street. All he had to do was turn and her condo was the third on the left. *Got to get there.* Every cell in his body worked frantically to propel him forward. He rounded the corner and saw what he most feared: Jimmy grabbing Emma. She was struggling against him, her tote bags full of groceries scattered on the deserted sidewalk. She was no match for his massive strength as he dragged her toward a nearby alley, his thick hand wrapped around her throat. She couldn't scream, could barely breathe. Xavier's blood ran cold.

"Jimmy!" Xavier shouted. "Stop!"

The man's massive head snapped up, as he focused on Xavier. He frowned, even as his grip on Emma's throat loosened and she screamed, frantically clutching at the man's massive forearm. Jimmy hesitated, obviously not wanting to let go of his victim, but after taking in Xavier's size and his speed, he must have thought better of holding on. Instead, he shoved Emma hard to the ground. She fell with her arms outstretched, but hit the ground hard on her palms and knees. Jimmy took off back down the street but his heavy frame meant he couldn't run that fast. Distantly, Xavier heard the siren of his detective friend. Thank God.

"Emma! You okay?" Xavier cried, stopping to help her up.

"Fine… I'm fine," she croaked, gently rubbing her neck. "Fine."

Xavier glanced up at Jimmy, who'd only made it about ten feet, but he clicked the remote on his key chain, opening up a car across the street. He was going to get away. That would not happen. Could not happen.

"I'll be right back," Xavier promised and sprinted to his feet, running as fast as his legs would carry him, taking the quickest route to Jimmy, who was in the middle of the street, just feet from his car door, when Xavier slammed into him and laid him flat on the ground. They fell in a tumble of limbs, and Xavier heard Jimmy's face hit the asphalt with a sickening crack. His nose maybe? But then the two men had tumbled to the ground, and Jimmy managed to pop up, arms swinging.

"You're going to regret that," he promised, wiping blood from his nose.

"I think you're going to be the one with regrets," Xavier promised. The sky opened up then and the rain came down, but Xavier hardly noticed. He was fixated on the large man in front of him. Not in shape, but heavy, and sometimes weight mattered more than muscle in a close fight.

Xavier had taken boxing lessons, so wasn't entirely out of his element. Plus, the man was going to be slower and tire easily. He jabbed and Xavier danced out of the way. Then Xavier swung, his right hook connecting at the man's chin, sending him backward. Jimmy lunged forward once more, but Xavier landed a hard blow to the man's stomach which sank him to his knees. A hard jab to the cheek toppled him then, even as the unmarked police car skidded to a stop in front of the men, lights flashing. Ian popped out of the driver's side, gun drawn.

"Hold it right there, asshole," he called to Jimmy. "Hands where I can see them."

Jimmy held his hands up, away from his bleeding face. Xavier backed away, hands up as well.

"Well, geez, X, looks like you didn't need me after all." Ian grinned. "Looks like you coulda handled this perp just fine."

"You better take him, Ian. 'Cause if you left him with me, I'd kill him."

Ian grabbed handcuffs from his back pocket. "Don't blame you," he agreed as he went about working Jimmy into a sitting position and handcuffing his wrists behind his back. "Jimmy, looks like you violated parole about eight ways to Sunday. You're going back for a long time."

"Fuck you," the man growled as he spat blood on the asphalt.

"Gotta love my job," Ian said. He glanced over Xavier's shoulder. "She okay?"

Xavier turned, to see Emma standing on the sidewalk, tears streaming down her face.

"I'll make sure she is," Xavier promised as he crossed the street and swooped her up in his arms. Tears flowed down her cheeks.

"I thought you… I just worried. Thank God you're okay," she cried, squeezing him hard.

"Me? I'm fine. I could handle ten of that jerk. No problem." Xavier squeezed her to his chest. "It's okay. He's going away for awhile, too. You don't have to be scared."

They watched together as Ian put him in his unmarked squad car. "Bring her down to the station for her statement, okay, X?" he called as he ducked into the driver's seat.

"Will do." Xavier kissed the top of Emma's head. "You going to be okay with that?"

She nodded into his chest.

Xavier drank the stale coffee at the police station as he sat beside Emma and listened to her recount the horror of the afternoon. With every new detail, he felt like he ought to have hit Jimmy one more time. The guy got off easy. Xavier held Emma's hand the entire time, squeezing it to let her know she wasn't alone and that he was there.

All he kept thinking was: *What if I'd stayed with the*

sexy woman from the train? If he'd done that, if he'd indulged, then what would have happened to Emma? Just the knowledge of how quickly things could've turned, how him *not* being there for her could've been such a disaster, made him feel sick with guilt. Yes, he'd made it on time. But he almost hadn't. And that was because of his stupid pursuit of…what? A pretty woman? Empty sex? Hadn't he been trying to fill the void inside him for more than a year with just sex with strangers?

He hadn't realized just how meaningless that life had been until he met Emma, until he felt the promise of something more. Now he realized that contentment couldn't be found in avoiding feelings. He'd just have to risk getting hurt, or not measuring up, or whatever love would ask of him, because he didn't want to live with the alternative: with Emma out of his life. When he thought about how Emma could've been hurt, all because he been too stubborn or too scared to admit that Emma was right, he wanted to hit himself. They did have a connection, a strong one, and he wasn't going to walk away from that.

The female officer across the desk finished taking her notes.

"Thanks for helping us," she told Emma. "I'll let you know if we need any more from you, but I think we're done for today. You have a ride home?" She glanced at Xavier.

"Yes," Xavier said. "I'll make sure she gets home."

She glanced at him, looking grateful, and as he sat

there, holding her hand, he realized for the first time about what his dad meant when he'd said, *Love isn't something you choose. It chooses you.* He realized then that he didn't want to live a life without Emma. He didn't want her on her own, walking down sidewalks by herself with people like Jimmy out there. He wanted to be there for her, in every way possible. For the first time, he started to think that love wasn't a prison, it was a gift. His father hadn't been a slave to his mother, he'd signed up to protect her, no matter how hard that task would be.

Xavier held Emma's hand as they walked out of the police station.

It wasn't far from her condo, so they opted to walk. The sun had set and the air had turned colder. The street lamps were bright, but even so, Xavier worried about her. He studied her profile, wondering if she was still scared, if she felt at all uneasy.

"Are you okay? Walking in the dark, I mean?" He squeezed her hand.

"With you? Of course. I saw your right hook," she teased, and he laughed a little. "Where did you learn to fight like that?"

"Boxing classes." He shrugged.

"Is your hand okay?" she asked him. He glanced down at his bruised knuckles. The split on his second knuckle had already begun to scab over. "I'm fine," he said, hardly feeling the pain anymore.

"Thank you, by the way," she said. "I didn't get a chance to thank you before. But you saved me. Thank you."

"Don't thank me." He glanced down at the sidewalk, looking at the dark, wet leaves. The rain had come and gone, but the sidewalks still glistened beneath the street-lights. "I should've been here with you. If I had stayed, none of this would've happened."

"I asked you to give up too much. I realize that now," she said. "But, it was worth a try. I thought…maybe." They neared her condo now and Xavier felt her tense as they walked past the very alley where Jimmy had hidden in wait. He felt furious and helpless all at the same time as he ushered her past that spot. Thank goodness he'd gotten there in time.

"I don't think I want to go home," Emma said and slowed. "I just… I'm not sure I can sleep there."

Xavier pulled her into his arms. "Come to my place, then. Stay the night. Hell, stay as long as you want."

"You'd let me?"

"I wouldn't have it otherwise," he said, and then flagged down a cab that happened to be headed down her street.

They slipped inside the cab and Xavier held Emma's hand tightly, realizing this was the first time he'd ever let a woman into his condo since Sasha. He'd had his share of one-night stands, but they all happened in hotel rooms or their places…or…he thought, thinking of the white-hot sex with Emma behind a condo building, right outside. But he didn't feel anxious at all. He wanted

Emma to see his place, wanted to invite her into his space and help her feel safe. It was the least he could do.

As they pulled up to his townhome in the west Loop, he paid the cab and then ushered her inside his brownstone. She stood in his foyer, eyes taking in his big staircase, his oversized living room and the granite island in his new kitchen.

"Wow," she said. "This is…beautiful." She noticed the pictures on his mantel above his wood-burning fireplace. The one old picture of his parents sat there, in the brown hues of the early 1980s.

"They look so happy," she said, studying the picture.

"Most of the time they weren't," he said, truthfully. "But sometimes, they were." He stood behind his couch, watching her. "That picture was taken before I was born. In fact, she was already pregnant with me at the time that was taken."

"Really?" Emma picked up the picture and studied it. Seeing her looking at the picture made him feel… understood somehow, though he couldn't figure out why.

"Are you hungry? Can I get you something to eat?" He asked her. "Maybe a drink? Some wine?"

"Is that what you tell all the girls you bring back here?" Emma joked, but the joke fell a little flat. There was too much jealousy in her voice.

"I don't invite anyone here."

Emma glanced up sharply.

"Not since Sasha," he said. "Wine?"

She nodded. He went to the kitchen and pulled out an

expensive Pinot from his wine rack. She stood, uncertainly, as he popped the cork and poured two glasses. She rubbed her arms and stood awkwardly in the center of his living room. "Maybe coming here…it was a mistake."

He froze, midpour. "What do you mean?"

Emma frowned. "Maybe I should go."

CHAPTER NINETEEN

EMMA SUDDENLY FELT CLAUSTROPHOBIC. Being with Xavier at his home, she felt closer to him than she ever had before. Plus, she still felt rattled about what nearly happened. Her fingers tingled still, the echoes of adrenaline. All she wanted was to be warm and safe, and yet nothing about Xavier felt like either. Not when he seemed so dead set against a relationship with her.

"I don't want you to go," he said, putting a glass of wine in front of her on the light granite countertop. She studied the wine.

"I'm so thankful that you saved me, but being here, near you, it's hard." It felt even harder to admit. *I care about you,* she wanted to shout. *Hell, I'm falling in love with you.* Being close to him but knowing that he wouldn't be faithful felt like a knife slicing through her heart. She was almost tempted to readjust her standards, try to work around his lack of commitment, but she knew, in the end, she couldn't. She wanted a man who'd love only her. She'd tried no commitment, but it just wasn't for her. She wanted more.

"Is it?" Xavier put down his own wineglass and moved closer to her. "Is it hard to be close to me?"

Emma felt her resolve melting now that Xavier was close enough to touch. She wanted to put her hands on his strong, flat chest, wanted to touch him. Even after everything she'd been through that evening, even with the aftershocks of adrenaline still thrumming in her veins, she felt the pull to him, the irresistible tug.

"I think we should talk," Xavier said. Emma glanced up into his hazel eyes, studying her in the low light of the dimmed kitchen. She swallowed, almost fearful of what he'd say.

"You don't have to explain." *I've heard enough,* is what Emma wanted to say. *I know all about you, about your limits.*

"I want to, though. After I left your place this morning, I..." He paused and took a sip of his wine. "I met a girl. On a train. I went back to her place."

Stricken, Emma froze, her hands clutching the edge of the granite countertop, suddenly feeling like it was the only thing holding her up. She imagined a beautiful woman leading Xavier into her bedroom, a scene probably repeated dozens of times, if not hundreds. She felt so unwanted then, so lacking. They'd had sex just the night before and then the very next day...he needed someone new? Of course women would fawn over him. *Look* at him, and yet, the fact that he accepted her invitation just made her feel a cold, base rejection.

"What then?" Emma's voice was low, barely a whisper. She'd asked the question, but she was almost positive she didn't want to hear the answer. She didn't want to hear about how he'd pleasured this woman, given her the best comes of her life, how he'd then come himself. Maybe in her mouth. Maybe inside her.

"All I could do was think of you," he admitted, eyes solemn as they met hers. "She wanted me, wanted to do things to me, but all I could do was think of you."

While you were fucking another woman, Emma thought bitterly.

"Did you make her come?"

He shook his head. "No," he said. "We only kissed. When I kissed her, I knew that she couldn't give me what I wanted. No one could give me what I wanted. No one except..." Xavier put down his wineglass and walked around the kitchen counter, now standing right next to her, so close, she could almost hear him breathing. "You. I want you, Emma Allaire."

She breathed in deeply, the spicy sweet smell of him, and felt a burst of hope light in her chest. "What are you telling me?"

He turned her to face him, and gently stroked her cheek.

"I'm falling in love with you. Actually, I'm in love with you already, Emma."

The words came as a shock, a surprise, like a bucket of cold water. What was he saying? Could it be true?

"You were right about me," he said, as he tucked a strand of blond hair behind her ear, his touch gentle, loving. "I was afraid I could never measure up to my father. To his dedication. I always thought it was because I didn't want to be weak, but I know he wasn't weak. Being faithful to my mother, that took real courage. Standing by her when she was sick, that wasn't weakness. It was strength."

"You don't have to be him. What he did for your mother, few could do." Emma couldn't break eye contact. She felt the warmth of Xavier's golden hazel eyes, the power in them, the magnetic pull.

"I probably can't be as strong as my father was, but I was afraid to even try," he said. "And when I think about how my fear hurt you…it makes me sick. Emma, if I'd stayed with that woman from the train, what could have happened to you? I could have really lost you."

Emma shuddered at the memory of Jimmy's rough hands on her, his big paw around her throat as he dragged her to a shadowy alley. The worst part had been the flat coldness of his eyes, the complete lack of humanity in them as he'd grabbed her. She swallowed, hard, and Xavier pulled Emma into his arms, squeezing her tightly.

"I want to make sure nothing bad ever happens to you, ever again," he promised, a murmur into her hair. She clung to him, hoping that was true, as a million emotions flooded her at once. "If you'll let me, I want to be your man. Your *only* man."

Emma pulled away and craned her neck to see Xavier's face, her heart tinged with doubt. This man who'd been so committed to casual sex, she just couldn't imagine him giving it all up. "Are you sure? But what about the boredom of relationships and how it makes people cheat."

"I think it does for most people," he said. "But you and I know we're not most people."

Xavier dipped down and laid a sensual kiss on her lips, a small gesture that sent a current of want down Emma's spine.

He broke the kiss. "You'll quit *Nost*?" Emma asked, still feeling dazed by Xavier's reversal. Could this be true? Could he really want to commit to her? Leave casual sex with strangers behind?

"I'm going to do more than quit *Nost*," Xavier promised. "I'm going to take it completely offline."

"But your business!" Emma cried.

Xavier shook his head. "I can make a new app," he said. "I don't want *Nost* up and running if a sexual predator like Jimmy can take advantage of it. I don't want a single woman terrorized like you were because of something I made. I'm taking it down and not putting it back up until I can either fix it or replace it with something better."

Emma realized Xavier was one hundred percent serious. "But just because one guy..."

"No," Xavier said, sounding emphatic. "I can't take the risk that anyone else will be hurt."

Emma nodded. She felt so proud of him suddenly, so full of love for this man. "But what about sex with strangers? I mean, won't you miss it?"

"Not if I get to have sex with you," he said, pulling her closer. "You are the best thing that's ever happened to me, Emma Allaire."

"I don't know what to say," she admitted.

"Say you'll be mine," Xavier murmured in her ear.

"Yes, *yes*, always," she said before he claimed her mouth once more.

EPILOGUE

One year later

XAVIER SAT AT the bar alone, drinking his scotch, when a beautiful redhead approached him, wearing a tight black miniskirt and a low-cut halter top. She was just his type: athletic, leggy, gorgeous smile.

"This seat taken?" she asked, smoky eyes never leaving him, as she signaled the bartender. She ordered a Hendrick's and tonic, as Xavier took in the curve of her long legs and the strappy stilettos she wore that just screamed sex. Look at those amazing muscles in her calves, and her small, round ass. Probably tight enough to bounce a quarter off of, he thought. She gave him a small, *come hither* smile, everything about her posture screaming, *I want to play.* The bartender set the drink down and she lifted it in her delicate hand. Her pink pouty lips took their first sip of her drink and Xavier imagined them wrapped around his cock. His groin grew hard then.

They sipped their drinks, neither one looking at the other, each one all too aware of the other.

Then the redhead leaned over. "I don't usually do this," she said to him. "But do you want to fuck?" She licked her lips to show the invitation was serious.

"Emma—" He stopped. He'd almost ruined their game, calling her by name. She was quick to intervene, shushing him with a single flick of her fingertip.

"No names, remember?"

"Right. I forgot." Emma had outdone herself this time, Xavier thought. The makeup, the wig…she looked like a different person. It thrilled him, the naughty game they played.

Emma slipped her hand in her purse and then retrieved a key card for a hotel room somewhere above them. She slapped it on the bar.

"Let's go upstairs," she murmured, voice low. "I've got a room."

"I don't usually do this," Xavier said, getting into the role, looking uneasy as he unbuttoned the top collar of his shirt.

"There's a first time for everything," she said. "That card is for you. I'll be waiting for you upstairs."

Emma slid off the stool, giving her red wig a pat with one hand, as she swayed her hips on her way to the elevator. Xavier would take her hard there, like he would a stranger, reliving the thrill of it all. He thought of the last year, of how he'd had Emma in so many ways, the hours they'd spent cuddling, getting to know one another, and now…the role play. They both worked together to find creative new ways to keep their sex sizzling. She truly was the perfect woman for him. He couldn't imagine sharing his life with another.

He slapped cash on the bar for the bartender and then slipped off his stool. Eager to join his "new" lover.

"You're a lucky man," the bartender told him, having overheard it all.

"You have no idea," Xavier said as he snatched the key card off the bar.

* * * * *